Finding Her C

By M.K. Ei

Finding Her Cyborg
By
M.K. Eidem
Turtle Point Publishing, Inc.
Copyright © 2022 by Michelle K. Eidem
Edited by: azedit@ziskoturtle.com

Synopsis

Talyani Zulfiqar has been an interplanetary superstar since she won the Worlds competition at thirteen. Her mother is a socialite of renowned beauty, and her father is a powerful Supreme Judge. From the outside, her life is perfect, but Taly had a secret and someone for whom she'd sacrifice everything.

Ranvir Somerled had been proud to serve and protect the people of Kirs as a member of the Cyborg Military Elite. Orphaned at a young age, it was the only family he had left. Then Emperor Shui, in his quest for power, destroyed that family, and Ranvir became a rebel.

With their world in chaos, can two drastically different people find a way to survive and maybe even love? Or will their secrets and misunderstandings tear them apart?

Prologue

Emperor Shui glanced around the large, multi-leveled auditorium on the palace grounds. It was the only space big enough to house all those attending the hearings. The emotions on the faces in the crowd ranged from shock and awe to fear and worry. He made a point to note which sections held people with the latter. They could be a part of the rebellion he'd failed to catch. No matter. He'd see to them later.

"Emperor Shui, we're ready when you are."

His top aide stood to the left of the large dais set up for Shui to preside over the hearings. Shui chuckled to himself at the thought. In his mind, the rebels were already convicted and condemned. A lesson needed to be learned, and he would teach it to all who'd thought to conspire against him.

"Let's start. Send them in," Shui instructed with a slight flick of his hand.

Outwardly, he retained a calm façade, but inside, his glee had him almost wanting to release a victorious cheer. Finally, he'd be rid of those who sought to betray him. By the end of the day, this lesson of retribution would resonate throughout the planet of Kirs and deter others from thinking about doing to him what the Cyborg Military Elite had almost managed.

To think how close to success they'd come caused his blood to boil. If that traitorous cyborg pod hadn't refused their orders, the medical techs doing the scans for a malfunction would not have discovered that many cyborgs were part of a rebellion to thwart his attempts to conquer the neighboring planet, Bionus. The evidence of their secret meetings and gatherings to exchange information had all been there on their closed network.

He seethed at the thought of being unable to hack into the other pods' closed networks. By the time he'd rounded up the cyborgs, intending to do just that, they'd scrubbed everything clean and had been smart enough to not leave anything on the mainframe.

The door to his right opened, letting in a long procession of rebels, primarily cyborgs wearing their prestigious uniforms. Uniforms that signified their roles as defenders of Kirs. But they hadn't defended Kirs. They'd betrayed their home planet and him with their actions.

Citizens of Kirs in plain clothes followed the cyborgs. The number of those about to receive judgment grew until rows and rows of rebels were gathered. Some stared at him with hateful glares, others murmured desperate pleas, while others had the audacity to look indifferent.

Hundreds of cyborgs from the Military Elite made up the rank of the rebels. Shui wasn't sure which ones remained loyal to him and who had taken part in growing the rebellion. He'd had their families tortured and their friends arrested, and he still couldn't determine the full scale of their plans.

Once the crowd settled, Shui stepped in front of the podium and activated the head mic he wore. "Today is a somber day for the world of Kirs. Rebels have been plotting against us. The men and women you see before you have been found guilty."

The crowd erupted with shouts of, "When were they given a trial?"

"Is this legal?"

"This isn't fair."

All caught his attention. With a pointed look at his aide, Shui signaled that he wanted those who'd openly posed those questions and remarks detained. The rebels were everywhere, and he would catch each and every one of them.

Shui put up both of his hands to silence the crowd. "As I said, these rebels have been found guilty of conspiring against the emperor and Kirs. They are hereby sentenced to prison for life."

Shui ignored another round of disruption from the onlookers and the shocked shouts thrown his way. His prime ministers, representing each country on Kirs, eyed him in dismay. They had been against his plans to take over Bionus and extend his reign as emperor over the small world from the beginning. They expected him to lead as his father had and settle for ruling only Kirs. But why would he when there was a vast number of planets that he could rule?

And he would. This was just a small bump in his road. If the Cyborg Military Elite soldiers had just done what they were supposed to, this would be behind him now.

Once more, Shui focused on the rebels he'd managed to catch. He wanted them to understand that he was judge, jury, and executioner. Their treachery had consequences.

The cyborgs didn't look so defiant, and the civilians appeared downright scared. They understood this would be a death sentence for many of them. While the cyborgs could withstand the hard labor, those without cybernetic enhancements wouldn't last long on Tyurma, Kirs' moon used to house prisoners.

With a nod from Shui, the prison officers from Tyurma, who'd come to collect the rebels, activated the remote-controlled hand and ankle cuffs. The ground shook from their heavy boots as the rebels turned toward the exit in unison. Then one-by-one the rebels, cyborgs and citizens alike, lined up and were guided toward the side door where they would receive their branding and board the prison transport.

The brand would be burned on their face, enabling Shui to find them anywhere if they ever escape Tyurma. He'd personally made sure the brand's specifications wouldn't allow the cyborgs' nanobots to heal their skin.

He hoped the "CR" for cyborg rebels and "R" for rebel brands would be clear on the holo-vids.

Shui realized he was smiling and quickly adjusted his expression to portray what he thought was a mournful look. This event was broadcast to all of Kirs, after all. He wanted to appear saddened by having to sentence so many of his people to life in prison.

The smile slid back into place, though, at the thought of what would happen to them, and no matter how hard he tried, he couldn't remove it from his face.

∞ ∞ ∞ ∞ ∞

Mayner huddled with a few of his fellow guards on the prison transport bound for Tyurma. They were successfully in space and far enough away from Kirs. "How soon before we need to take our leave?"

Kaza glanced fearfully over his shoulder. No one else was present in the corridor besides the three of them. "According to the instructions, evacuation of the transport should begin in another fifteen minutes. The emperor made it clear that there is no way to stop the explosions set onboard."

Mayner and Goran exchanged a look. They were cousins by marriage, and both had vowed they would not hesitate to get off this doomed transport when it came time. They sympathized with the cyborgs and other Kirsians because the emperor's actions were wrong, but only a fool would say that aloud.

"It's hard to imagine Emperor Shui had no intention of sending them to the prison colony," Kazan continued with a remorseful look.

"Let's get back to our stations," Goran said, the fear on his face very real. "I want to be ready when the time comes. The explosions will destroy the transport and all those on board. I have no intentions of being left behind to die."

As the three rushed off, none knew the cyborgs being escorted to their cell several corridors away. Their enhanced hearing enabled them to hear the guards' words clearly. While not in the same pod group, the five cyborgs all wore grim expressions from what they'd learned.

They would not have a chance to escape Tyurma as they'd thought. They would not have an opportunity to return to Kirs and see their families. The emperor had consigned them to death if what they'd heard was true. When they reached their designated cell, the guard shoved all of them into the enclosed space. There were a few jeers and taunts to which none of them responded.

Once alone, the tallest of the group faced the others. "We've been set up. The emperor had no intentions of giving us a fair trial, and now he dooms us to death with the lie that we were bound to Tyurma."

Another took up speaking, "He has condemned everyone onboard. Our friends, our fellow cyborgs."

The other three gazed forward, brows creased as if in deep thought. They were eerily similar in appearance with dark hair and narrow-set eyes. The one in the middle shifted his gaze to encompass all of them and spoke, "We must put aside whatever differences or trust issues we have at this moment and save our brethren. I have family bound to Tyurma on this vessel."

A moment of silence, and then they all replied simultaneously, "Agreed."

The tallest cyborg volunteered to open his mainframe and broadcast the warning. They now were down to seven minutes before the alleged explosions would detonate. Messages were sent within pod groupings until the vast majority were aware.

They were out of time.

The revolt needed to start now.

Chapter One

Ten years earlier

"Rock. Ranvir. You go right. Nas, you're with me," Major Reiji Demeter quietly ordered into his mouthpiece.

Two soldiers peeled off the formation, heading down the corridor their commander had indicated.

Reiji hated this type of mission. Pirates had taken control of the civilian transport, The Giles, and it was his job and the job of the elite soldiers he commanded to reclaim it with no loss of life. Except for those of the pirates, and therein was the problem. In a straight-out fight, it would only take minutes to neutralize the intruders, but with civilians on board, they had to take special precautions because civvies never reacted well to blaster fire.

They'd already taken down the pirates who had taken over the ship's control center, more than a dozen of them, but their captain was still unaccounted for. The coward had taken off for the passenger section as soon as Reiji's team had boarded, hoping the taking of hostages would save his life.

It wouldn't because Reiji didn't negotiate with pirates. They would either surrender or die, preferably with no additional loss of life.

He and Nas turned a corner, their blasters already raised, then immediately stilled. The pirate captain stood halfway down the corridor, holding a trembling female in front of him. The tip of his blaster pressed against her temple.

"I want safe passage back to my ship, or this bitch dies!" he screamed at them.

Reiji's answer was to put a perfect smoking hole between his eyes. Slowly, the pirate fell back, pulling the female with him.

"Nice shot," Nas commented, his eyes scanning for other possible threats as they moved forward.

"Target down," Reiji spoke into his mic, ignoring Nas's statement. "Stay alert in case we missed one."

"Affirmative, Major."

The female rolled away from the dead pirate and then hurried down the corridor to an open door. It sealed as Nas called out, "Wait."

"Leave her," Reiji ordered, tilting his head to listen as a transmission came through on his secure line. "Shit."

"What's wrong?" Nas's gaze shot back to him.

"Rock. Ranvir. Continue your sweep. Nas and I will be going to the Premier Suite."

"Copy that, Major."

Spinning on his heel, Reiji made his way to the main lift.

"What's going on?" Nas asked, following close behind.

"The family of a Supreme Judge is on this ship."

"What?! What are they doing off-planet? Especially without an escort?"

"Don't know, but now we have to verify their well-being, then babysit them until a fully armed escort arrives."

"Wonderful," Nas muttered.

∞ ∞ ∞ ∞ ∞

The Premier Suite took up the whole upper level of the ship and was accessed through a private elevator with a code generated by the current occupant. There was a military override, which Reiji received before boarding The Giles. Entering the lift, Reiji opened a concealed panel. After swiping his override card, he input the twenty-five-digit master code into the tiny numeric keypad, which sent the elevator directly up to the Premier Suite.

As the doors opened, he and Nas took up defensive positions. There was little chance that a pirate had made it this far, but that didn't mean there wasn't some untrained, trigger-happy idiot with a blaster inside, ready to shoot first and ask questions later.

Luckily, there wasn't.

They quickly cleared the first lavish room, then moved on to the next, the next, the next, and the next.

"How many frigging rooms can this place have?" Nas muttered.

Reiji didn't reply. Instead, he pulled out a handheld unit from the storage pocket on his outer leg and began scanning the walls.

"What are you doing?"

"It's common for these luxury suites to have escape rooms for their occupants to hide in and evacuate from if necessary. This one is... right here," he said as the handheld began to beep excitedly. Using a fist, he pounded on the wall. "This is Major Reiji Demeter of Kirs Elite Planetary Defense Force. This ship is now secure. It's safe for you to disengage the room's locks."

It took several long moments during which they retracted the visors on their helmets, but finally, the sound of locks disengaging and seals releasing was heard. The door slowly opened.

"Shit!" Reiji cursed as an elegantly dressed woman stepped out. Her white-blonde hair was artfully arranged around a heart-shaped face with big brown eyes, a petite nose, and enhanced red lips. "I should have known."

"Hello, Reiji."

"What the fuck are you doing in space, Pooja?" he demanded. "You hate space."

"It's *Lady Zulfiqar* to *you*, Major Demeter," she told him haughtily.

"Ah yes, that's all you ever wanted to be now, isn't it, Pooja? To be considered a 'Lady' instead of the dirty D-Twelver you are."

Her arrogant façade faded, and she snapped, "I *am* a Lady!"

He sneered. "And all it took for you to achieve that was to divorce me and abandon our son."

"I never..."

"Hello, Mother, or do I need to address you as Lady Zulfiqar, too?" Nas asked, stepping into her line of sight.

"I... what... who... Nasli?" she stammered, the color draining from her face.

"So, you do remember me. I'm surprised since your current husband successfully erased you from every document that connected us."

"He did that to protect me. He..."

"He did it to protect himself," Reiji spat out. "So he could be elected Supreme Judge because we all know that never would have happened if it was discovered his wife not only came from District Twelve but gave birth to one."

"Why is that man calling you mother?"

The young voice had all three heads turning. A young girl emerged from the escape room. Her long white-blonde hair was pulled back by two decorative combs, framing her crystal blue eyes and an elegant little nose perfectly centered in her heart-shaped face.

Pooja recovered her composure. "This doesn't concern you, Talyani. Get back inside until I say you can come out."

Swinging his blast rifle around to his back, Nas removed his helmet, exposing short white-blonde hair that matched hers as he went down on one knee. "I call her mother because that's what she is, which means you're my half-sister."

"Stop!" Pooja shrieked, but everyone ignored her.

"Really? I always wanted a brother." Talyani's wide gaze looked up to Pooja. "Why didn't you tell me I had one, Mother?"

"I…"

"Well, you know now." Pulling off his tactical glove, he extended his hand to her. "I'm Nasli. Nasli Demeter."

Talyani didn't even hesitate to slip her much smaller hand into his. "It's very nice to meet you, Nasli. I'm Talyani Zulfiqar."

"Nice to meet you, too. So, Little Sis, what are you doing out here in deep, dark space?"

"I've been chosen to compete at Worlds."

Nas knew Worlds was a competition, held every five years, between the eleven countries on Kirs for bragging rights on who had the most talented, beautiful, and intelligent citizens. Winners became national heroes. And the losers? Well, no one ever heard of them again. Why anyone would want to compete in such a thing, let alone allow their child to, was beyond Nas's comprehension.

"What does that have to do with you being in space?" Nas asked.

"Mother wanted us to go to Bionus because of their enhancing treatments. Mother said I needed one before I competed."

Nas glared at his mother, who just sniffed and raised her chin slightly. He turned back to his sister. "I'm sure you didn't need any of that."

"That's what my father said, but mother insisted. So, we went." She looked to her mother, then leaned in closer to Nas as if sharing a secret. "I was only with my consultant for an hour. She showed me how to apply enhancements so my eyes would stand out on stage."

"I see. What are you competing in?"

"Vocal," she told him proudly. "I love to sing."

"I'm sure you're very good."

She gave a little shrug. "People tell me I am, so I guess we'll see."

"That's enough." Pooja put a hand on Talyani's shoulder, pulling her away from her newly found brother. "If the ship is secure, I want you both to leave. NOW."

"But, Mother..."

"Quiet, Talyani."

Nas didn't like how his mother's hand tightened on his half-sister's shoulder, but as the wife of a Supreme Judge, he had to obey her. Keeping his eyes locked with his mother's, he slowly rose. Pulling on his tactical glove, he swung his rifle around, letting its muzzle remain on her for a moment before aiming it at the deck. The widening of her eyes let him know he'd made his point.

"Let's go, Nas." When Nas didn't move, Reiji hardened his voice. "Lieutenant! Now!"

That had Nas moving, but when they reached the lift, he looked behind him to find his mother and half-sister had followed them and knew he had one more thing to say. "I'll make sure to watch your performance, Little Sis."

"Really?" Her eyes sparkled with excitement.

"Really." With that, he left.

One month ago

Talyani hurried towards her father's office. She'd been working in her private wing of her parents' estate when the news report came across the music channel she'd been listening to. She knew it had to be false. She just needed her father to verify it.

Some thought it was strange she still lived on her parents' estate. After all, she'd won the Worlds vocal competition at thirteen. Since then, she had become the most popular vocalist on Kirs and their closest neighbor, Bionus, where she traveled several times a year to perform.

It wasn't that she didn't have enough credits to purchase her own estate. As Supreme Judge, her father's security rivaled that of the emperor's, and she needed that because she had some rabid fans.

She knew this was a bad time of day to interrupt her father, and his assistant was going to block her, but she'd long ago learned how to get around that pesky man.

Slipping out through a set of glass doors, she made her way along the stone terrace curved along this side of the estate, including her father's office. As she approached the clear doors that led into his private office, she discovered they were already open and heard the raised voices inside.

"But, Badar..."

"No, Pooja, there's nothing I can do."

"But he's my son!"

"Keep your voice down. Do you know what I had to do to ensure no one ever discovered that? Do you want me, *us*, to lose everything for which we've worked? Our standing? Our home? Think what would happen to Talyani."

"I know, and I don't want anything to change either, but isn't there something you can do? You're a Supreme Judge, for God's sake."

"Which is why I can't do anything. The emperor isn't just gathering up cyborgs, Pooja. He's gathering up their entire family and any friends he even thinks might sympathize with them. He means to send them to Tyurma."

Her mother's eyes widened. "What?! But that means...."

Her father sighed and shoved a hand through his hair. "Now, do you understand why there can't be even the slightest hint you have a son that's a cyborg?"

"Yes, Badar." Her mother deflated as if all the air had been sucked from her.

"You need to vocally support the emperor whenever you are out. Whether it's dress shopping, having lunch, or just walking down the street. He needs to be assured we stand by him and only him."

Her mother nodded eagerly. "Yes, Badar. I can do that."

"You have to, or we're all dead, including Talyani. Not even her fame will save her if Shui discovers she is the half-sister of a cyborg."

Talyani couldn't believe what she was hearing. The news report was *right*? The emperor *had* recalled the Cyborg Military Elite and was incarcerating them. Not just them but their family and friends.

And her parents were planning on supporting him even though they knew it was wrong. Spinning to leave, she inadvertently caused a pebble to strike a pane of glass in the door.

"Who's out there?"

Hearing her father's footsteps quickly moving toward the opened door, she reached into her pocket and pulled out the earbuds she always carried. Sticking them in her ears, she bobbed her head up and down as if listening to something.

"Talyani?" When she didn't respond, he touched her shoulder.

Shrieking, Talyani quickly spun around and dramatically grasped her chest. "Father! You startled me."

His brows lowered, and he scanned the area behind her. "What are you doing out here?"

"I was coming to see you but knew Zau wouldn't let me in, so I took my 'special' way." She gave him a smile she knew he could never resist. "But then Kru sent me this new arrangement for my latest disk, and I couldn't wait to listen to it. You know how I am."

"I do." Relaxing, he gave her an indulgent look.

"Do you have time to chat?" She glanced behind her father. "Oh, hello, Mother. Am I interrupting something?"

Her mother brushed an imaginary piece of lint from her sleeve. "No, dear, of course not. Your father and I were just discussing some upcoming social events."

Talyani feigned surprise. "How funny, that's what I was coming to discuss with Father."

"You were?" he asked.

"Yes, I wanted to let you know I scheduled my next concert on Bionus, so I'll be going off-planet in the next few weeks."

He grimaced and shook his head. "Oh, baby, I'm not sure that's a good idea right now."

"Why, Father?" Her crystal blue eyes widened in confusion. "Is there something going on I don't know about?"

"Of course not," he immediately replied.

"Then I need to fulfill my contract. Otherwise, I'll owe the promoter an obscene number of credits."

"Yes. Well, we can't have that," he agreed.

"Well, I just wanted you to know. If you'll excuse me, I want to listen to this arrangement again. Hopefully, I'll be able to debut it on Bionus."

∞ ∞ ∞ ∞ ∞

Returning to her suite, Talyani began to pace. What was she going to do? She couldn't let Shui send her half-brother to Tyurma. After meeting Nas all those years ago, her mother swore Taly to secrecy, telling her it would upset her father if he ever found out they'd met.

She hadn't understood it then, but she'd obeyed her mother and never mentioned it. That didn't mean she hadn't kept in touch with Nas.

At first, she wasn't sure how to do it, but after winning Worlds, she requested to perform for the soldiers who'd saved her, and her request was granted. During the concert, she'd been able to slip Nas a secure comms code. It allowed them to communicate and be involved in each other's lives, although Talyani always revealed more about her life than her brother ever did.

After his father died, Nas would only say it was because of a cluster fuck. He'd also talked even less. For months Talyani hadn't heard from him. She and the rest of Kirs were told their space forces had encountered a previously unknown species with deadly consequences, but their forces had been victorious. Those lost were honored as heroes.

Nas's name hadn't been on that list.

Still, she hadn't heard from him. She'd been ready to go to her father for help when Nas finally reached out.

During the alien confrontation, he'd been badly wounded and decided to enter the Cyborg program. If she thought he'd been distant before, now it felt as if there was a universe between them. He only ever contacted her on her birth day to wish her well, then would disconnect. None of that mattered, though. He was her brother, and she wouldn't let him die on Tyurma.

She just needed to figure out how to prevent it.

Chapter Two

Talyani couldn't believe she'd done it. She'd been able to sneak onto one of the Tyurma prison ships. It had been easier than she thought since the emperor had demanded everyone attend or watch his sham of a trial. It left no one to guard the ships.

She looked like every other guard in her drab green shirt, pants, and black lace-up boots. It had taken a great deal of work, but she'd finally been able to restrain her signature hair beneath a cap the guards wore.

From the information she'd gathered, the prisoners were to be loaded in order of their unit designation, which meant Nas would be on the second ship. She quickly moved to the cell-level control room and found the perfect hiding place.

A maintenance closet.

It had evenly spaced slats near the top for air circulation, and with her height, she could see out perfectly. She needed to watch which cell the controller assigned Nas's pod and what security code he used to seal them in.

Simple.

Nothing could possibly go wrong.

Right?

In what seemed like a lifetime later, she leaned back against a side wall. Had something gone wrong? Had the cyborgs been found not guilty? Had all this been for nothing?

No.

She knew Shui. He wasn't going to change his mind. He wasn't that benevolent. He wanted the cyborgs gone. So, they would be gone, and no one had the power to stop him.

Hearing voices, she straightened and peered through the slats.

A guard walked into the room, and after pushing several buttons on the control console, he ordered, "Group 146. Cell 225."

"Move it, you traitors!" A guard from outside the control room barked.

Talyani covered her mouth to muffle her gasp as she saw a group of cyborgs move past the large viewing window that faced the cells, their cheeks branded with the letters "CR." Her father hadn't said anything about *that*.

The control room guard pushed several buttons again. "Cell 225 secure. Group 147, Cell 226," the guard ordered, and she saw another group pass, this one filled with civilians, and their cheeks were branded, too, but with the letter "R."

This went on and on. Some groups she saw, some she didn't. But she saw the guard in the control room repeatedly touching the same buttons.

"Group 371. Cell 450." Talyani's breath quickened. That was her brother's group. "Cell 450 secured. That's it. We're full. Send the rest to the next ship."

With that, the guard left the room. Talyani had to force herself to wait and not immediately jump out of her hiding place to release her brother. If she made a mistake now, Nas would be instantly recaptured.

No, she had to wait until they were close enough to Tyurma for her plan to work.

Feeling the vibration beneath her feet, she spread her legs wide and braced herself for takeoff.

∞ ∞ ∞ ∞ ∞

Major Ranvir Somerled stared at his clenched fists as he sat in his holding cell. They'd been so close to stopping the emperor. So close to preventing the needless slaughter of millions of innocent lives on Bionus because of the emperor's hunger for power.

Instead, he was on his way to prison, and the rebellion was dead. Lifting his head, he assessed the other four occupants in the cell. One was a gangly civilian who cupped his branded cheek and sobbed. He couldn't be more than twenty.

The other three were dressed like him in the black-trimmed, grey uniforms that all cyborgs wore. None of them were part of the pod he'd commanded, so he couldn't use his closed network to talk to them, and he refused to use the open network because the emperor would be monitoring it.

His gaze returned to the civilian. "Why are you here?"

Ranvir kicked the other man's foot when he got no response, causing the man to shriek.

"What?" he sobbed, his terrified gaze shooting to Ranvir. "What do you want?"

"Why are you here?" Ranvir repeated. He wouldn't put it past the emperor to insert a civilian spy into their group, knowing how protective cyborgs were of them.

"I... I'm a communications specialist," he stuttered. "I forwarded messages between rebels."

"Cyborgs don't need their 'messages' forwarded," Ranvir growled.

"Non-cyborgs do." The civilian dragged his shirt sleeve over his face to wipe away the snot and tears. When he hit his new facial enhancement, he winced, "Fuck, that hurts."

Ranvir ignored him and turned his attention to the other cyborgs. "Are any of you members of the same pod?"

The three silently looked at him before the largest one spoke. "No."

The other two shortly followed.

"No."

"No."

"Can any of you link with your pods?" Ranvir asked.

Again, he received a chorus of noes.

"They're separating us in the hope it will weaken us. It won't." But Ranvir knew it could.

During Shui's sham of a trial, he'd been able to communicate with the other members of his pod through their closed network, but then one by one, he'd lost them.

That meant they were either dead or out of the closed network's range. The cyborg part of his brain calculated the odds and was sure it was the second, but the human part worried it could be the first because Emperor Shui had lost his mind.

Through his boots, he felt the vibration of the engines starting up. He leaned back against the wall, gripping the bench with the back of his knees, and braced for takeoff.

∞ ∞ ∞ ∞ ∞

"What are you doing?!" The exclamation stilled Taly's hand as she was about to push open the door of her hiding place.

"I forgot the visual of my family." The guard hurried across the room to rip the visual off the view screen.

"You're willing to lose your life over a *visual*?!" the other guard sputtered.

"It's the last one taken where my father was still alive," he defended, stuffing it into his jacket.

"I still say you're an idiot. Now can we get to our escape pod? I want to be as far away as possible when this ship explodes."

"Calm down. We still have fifteen minutes before we can launch. The emperor wants the ships close enough, so the explosion is seen from Kirs, but far enough away, so the debris won't cause any damage."

Talyani stood in stunned silence as the guards left the room.

She couldn't have heard what she thought she had, could she?

Was the ship really going to explode?

Had the emperor planned to murder these people all along?

Oh, Gods, she needed to get off this ship!

Everyone needed to get off this ship.

Shoving open the door, she rushed to the control console. Shaking, she reached out only to curl her trembling fingers back.

Oh, Gods. What was the code?

Closing her eyes, she took a deep breath and calmed herself down. Deep breath in then out, just as she did every time before going on stage. After a moment, everything settled, and she recalled the code.

Opening her eyes, she took in the console. All the cells had been open when the prisoners arrived, but the guard had closed them individually. There had to be a way to open them all at once.

Then she saw it. Along the top of the console, similar to what her sound engineer used during concerts to control the vast number of speakers, was each cell's number listed individually and the large icon that synced them all. Every cell number lit up when she pressed it. She entered the code she'd seen the guard use and pressed enter.

The cell doors started to open. Perfect! She rushed out of the control room to cell 450 and her brother.

∞ ∞ ∞ ∞ ∞

Ranvir was immediately on his feet and ready to fight when the energy bars to their cell doors suddenly disappeared. So were the other cyborgs. They weren't anywhere near Tyurma. There was no reason for their cells to be opened yet. Unless the guards were coming to kill them, they wouldn't find that so easy since the wrist and ankle cuffs that had restrained them during the trial had been removed when they entered the cell.

Ranvir was more than ready to defend himself. However, he wasn't prepared for the beauty who rushed into the cell in an ill-fitting guard's uniform and a cockeyed hat, strands of white hair escaping from it. Her striking blue eyes quickly scanned the cell.

"Where's Nas?" she demanded urgently.

"Who?" one of the other cyborgs asked.

"Nas," she snapped, her lyrical voice becoming sharp. "Captain Nasli Demeter. He's supposed to be in this cell."

Ranvir knew who Nas was. He had served with him under his father and then under Nas when he'd taken over the unit. After entering the cyborg program, he'd even been a part of Nas's pod. Until the day he'd been promoted to a major and assumed command of his own pod.

It wasn't common for a cyborg to promote out of a pod. Pods were tight-knit groups, but Nas had put him up for promotion, stating Ranvir was a natural leader and his talent and skill would be wasted if he wasn't leading a pod.

When promoted, Ranvir severed his closed-network link with every member of his old pod, except for Nas. They'd served together for too long and decided to maintain the network, even though they rarely used it. Tapping into it now, Ranvir reached out to Nas and received no response.

"My Gods! You're Talyani," the civilian blurted out, his voice full of awe. "*The* Talyani. I'm Vujcec. Vujcec Wells. I'm a huge fan."

Talyani's gaze went to the man she hadn't noticed before sitting on one bench. Ranvir could tell she was used to being recognized. Still *really*? On a prison transport ship?

"Captain Demeter is not on this ship," Ranvir responded, causing her gaze to jerk back to his.

Her eyes widened in disbelief, and she took a step forward. "What? He has to be. My source told me they were loading you by your unit numbers."

"Your source was wrong," he told her bluntly. "They made sure to separate the pods."

"Oh, Gods, what do I do now?" Talyani ran a shaking hand through her hair. "He needs to get off whatever ship he's on, or he's going to die. We all will."

"What are you talking about?!" Ranvir gripped her waist and slammed her against the cell wall. He forced himself to ignore how light and delicate she felt or how her waist was so tiny that his hands encircled it.

Talyani cried out and gasped for breath. Ranvir ignored his remorse for the rough handling. "Explain!" he repeated, his fingers digging deeper into her flesh.

"The...the ships are set to self-destruct," she finally managed to get out.

"What?!" Wells shrieked, but everyone ignored him.

Holding her gaze, Ranvir demanded, "When?"

"In... in less than fifteen minutes," she stuttered. "I overheard two of the guards talking about it." Her gaze searched his. "Are you sure Nas isn't on this ship?"

He was certain. "I'm sure."

"Then we need to get word to him." She struggled in his hold, but his grip remained firm.

"We'd have to use the open network," one of the other cyborgs said.

"Then do it!" she demanded, looking over his shoulder.

Ranvir lowered her to her feet. "The emperor will know the minute we use the open network. He'll immediately destroy the ships, and no one will survive."

Suddenly all four cyborgs stiffened. They stared straight ahead, unblinking.

"What?" She grabbed his shirt and shook him. "What's going on?"

He blinked and focused on her face. "Someone else has discovered the plot. He's broadcasting the information over the open network. The explosion can't be altered."

Ranvir looked to the other cyborgs, who nodded. "Let's go."

∞ ∞ ∞ ∞ ∞

Minutes later, Talyani had her breath knocked out of her again as she was shoved into a seat in an escape pod. Her stomach struggled to settle after being slung over a cyborg's shoulder as they'd raced through the corridors.

How they'd made it through the crush of bodies, she couldn't say, but they had. At least she and the four cyborgs had. She didn't know what had happened to her 'fan.'

Instead of immediately closing the door, which would launch the escape pod, the gruff cyborg who had carried her moved to the control console.

"What are you doing?" she asked when she could finally speak.

Instead of answering, his fingers rapidly moved over the controls.

"Hurry up," one of the other cyborgs growled.

Ranvir ignored both of them. He wasn't the computer expert of his pod, so the reprogramming of their destination and deactivation of their transponder was taking longer than he'd like. Still, it was better than being sent directly back to Kirs.

"Done," he announced. "Launch us."

"Wait!" Running as fast as he could toward them was her fan. "Don't leave me!"

The cyborg's hand didn't pause.

"Stop!" she exclaimed. "You can't leave him!"

His hand stilled for only a moment, but it was enough for the fan to dive beneath the door before it sealed and the escape pod launched.

"Thank Gods," Vujcec breathed as he rolled onto his back. "I thought you were going to leave me."

"We were," Ranvir informed him. "You're of no use to us."

"And *she* is?" Vujcec jabbed a thumb towards Talyani as he stood. "Why? Because she's a woman? I thought they removed *that* part when you became a cyborg so you wouldn't be distracted."

"*She* is the one who freed us from our cell," Ranvir told him coldly. "If it weren't for *her*, we'd all still be sealed in our cells. That's why she's here. You have done nothing but snivel and cry for all your claims of assisting the rebellion."

All four cyborgs looked to the viewing port at the same time.

"Strap in and brace for impact," Ranvir ordered, taking the seat beside Talyani.

Chapter Three

Talyani had experienced turbulence before. You couldn't travel in space as much as she did and not. But that was like comparing the gentle waves on a beach to a series of tidal waves. Five, to be exact. One for each ship that exploded. Each wave tossed and rolled the escape pod. At one point, she was sure none of them would survive. Her head slammed back against the hull during one particularly violent roll, and darkness descended. She welcomed it.

∞ ∞ ∞ ∞ ∞

"Why are you sending us there?"

Ranvir released his seat restraint and then checked to make sure Talyani still had a pulse before looking at the cyborg who questioned him. The sleeve of their uniforms revealed that two were lieutenants and the other was a private, but nothing else.

"Names. Specialties," Ranvir ordered, and they instantly responded to his authority.

"Pike. Weapons specialist." The brown-haired lieutenant immediately replied.

"Tane," the private spoke next. "Navigator."

"Ganesha." A deep well of a voice came from the larger lieutenant. "Pilot."

They didn't give him their first names, but Ranvir hadn't expected it, as first names were only used within a pod.

"I'm Somerled. The coordinates I entered are beyond the empire's normal flight paths. It gives us time to decide where we want to go."

"There's a tracker," Pike informed him.

"Which I disabled before we launched. They'll have to do in-depth scans to locate us now, which won't be possible until the debris fields dissipate. That's going to take a long time with five destroyed ships. By then, we should be long gone."

"We're not returning to Kirs?" Tane asked.

"No," Ranvir told him, realizing that Tane was relatively young for a cyborg. "The Rebellion is lost, Private. At least for now."

"Then where are we going?" Tane pressed. "Escape pods have a limited range."

"Bionus," Pike suggested.

"The planet Shui's about to invade?" Ranvir looked at him in disbelief.

"We'll assist them," Pike argued.

"Four cyborgs against the entire Kirs military?" Ranvir just shook his head. How the hell had these two ever been selected for the Elite program?

"Tuater," Ganesha said.

Finally, an intelligent suggestion. Tuater was a small planet on the outer edge of the Leonis Star System. It would be an excellent choice if they were in an actual ship, not an escape pod. "We'll never make it in this."

"Go to Tyurma," Talyani murmured, lifting a hand to the back of her head.

"And do what?" Tane sneered. "Turn ourselves in? How stupid are you?"

Talyani glared unflinchingly into the cyborg's mocking gaze. "Stupid enough to sneak onto a ship bound for Tyurma. Stupid enough to obtain the codes that set you free." Talyani's words grew louder as she released her harness and stood, bringing her closer to the cyborg. "Do you think I planned all that and didn't have a way for Nas to escape?"

Silence reigned in the pod as Talyani continued to stare Tane down.

"You always planned on going to Tyurma?" Ranvir's question pulled her blue gaze to him.

"Not to the moon itself, but to the waystation on its dark side where the prison supply ships dock. My private ship has been there for 'repairs' the last two weeks." Her fingers made air quotes. "I'd already bribed the guards to take Nas and his pod to the station. Once they were on board, we were going to fly to Bionus. The flight plan was approved weeks ago, so it wouldn't raise any suspicions. Once I was on Bionus, they'd take off for parts unknown, and I'd report my ship stolen."

"You actually believed that would work?" Pike snorted.

"Yes." Ranvir could tell she believed that. "And it would have if Shui hadn't decided to be judge, jury, and executioner."

"But he did," Ranvir told her. "Now, you can't return to Kirs either."

"What?" He saw the slightest sliver of doubt enter her eyes for the first time. "What do you mean? No one knows I'm involved."

"They will once our escape pod docks and your ship takes off," he informed her.

"Shit," she whispered and dropped back into her seat. The reality of her situation had started to sink in.

Ranvir turned to the console and entered the new coordinates.

∞ ∞ ∞ ∞ ∞

Talyani watched as the cyborg with the major's insignia on his arm skillfully maneuvered the escape pod into the docking port closest to her ship on the way station.

She'd thought she'd prepared for all contingencies. Her ship had a 'technical' problem that allowed it to dock at the way station. The crew had transported down to the moon's surface to witness the trial since there wasn't live reception on the dark side of Tyurma. She'd planned on sneaking Nas and his pod on board before her crew returned. They'd then travel on to Bionus as scheduled. That wasn't going to be possible now.

"Be ready," The major ordered, and the other cyborgs took up defensive positions in front of the hatch, shoving her and Vujcec behind them.

"Ready for what?" she asked.

"Whatever's on the other side," he told her, joining the others. "Pike, open the hatch."

She watched as the hazel-eyed cyborg, with the regulation cut of short brown hair, slapped the button, and the door slid open, revealing...

Nothing.

No one was there.

"Move out," the major ordered.

"Everyone is on the surface for Shui's transmission," Talyani told them as they exited the escape pod into an eerily silent corridor. The other waystations she'd been on were busy, boisterous places filled with people.

None of the cyborgs responded to her comment. They continued to walk forward in formation, forcing her and Vujcec to follow.

"My Gods, that's an MKX-7!" Vujcec exclaimed as they passed a viewport. "You own an MKX-7?!"

"It's the ship Nas recommended," she responded absently, her gaze remaining on the major.

When they reached the airlock where her ship berthed, she pushed forward to enter the code to open it. The major got there first and, to her amazement, could disengage the lock.

"How the hell were you able to do that?" she demanded angrily.

"Override code," he told her, moving through the airlock to the ship's hatch and entering the code again, received a different result.

"That's not going to work." This time, she got past the other cyborgs and entered a long combination of numbers and symbols. At the major's raised eyebrow, she shrugged. "Nas suggested the extra layer of security, especially when the ship is left unattended. I was on a hijacked ship once."

"I know. I was part of the rescue team," he told her.

"You were?" she asked as the ship's hatch opened. "I don't remember seeing you."

"Because you didn't," he bit out, then gestured. "Let's go."

∞ ∞ ∞ ∞ ∞

Ranvir's jaw clenched as they made their way to the bridge. He couldn't believe he'd revealed that. Cyborgs rarely discussed missions outside of the team or pod that completed them. For some reason, he needed her to know.

He remembered everything about that mission, including how Nas and Reiji had acted after finding the Supreme Judge's family. He'd known something had happened but never discussed it.

Now he knew why.

Nas had met Talyani and became obsessed. By all appearances, she was just as obsessed with Nas. After all, she'd purchased the sleekest, fastest, most expensive ship available on his recommendation.

On the bridge, he and the other cyborgs quickly and efficiently prepared the ship for departure. Glancing at Talyani and Wells, he pointed to seats along the hull. "Sit and strap in."

"Troubadour, this is Tyurma Waystation. You are not cleared for departure," a voice stated over the comms. Five pairs of eyes looked at Talyani.

"It's an old term for a traveling singer," she explained. "It seemed appropriate."

"Troubadour, I repeat, you are not cleared for departure. Shut down your engines."

Ranvir silenced the transmission, then looked to Ganesha in the pilot's seat. "Get us out of here."

"Yes, Major." Ganesha disconnected the airlock and guided the ship away from the station using the thrusters. When they were a safe distance out, he engaged the main engines. In moments, Tyurma disappeared behind them.

"Shit," Ganesha muttered. "This girl can move."

Ranvir ignored Ganesha's comment and looked to Tane in the navigator's chair. "Anyone pursuing us?"

"No, Major. All radar hits are on the other side of Tyurma. Gods, I haven't even heard rumors about a navigation system this advanced. It not only detects vessels at this range but identifies them by name. There are shuttles out there besides escape pods."

Ranvir just grunted. "Make sure it stays that way. Super detection and speed do us no good without a defense system."

"We have a defense system," Talyani informed him from where she sat next to Wells.

Ranvir slowly turned to glare at her. "As well equipped as the MKX-7 is for defending against pirates, it doesn't stand a chance against a military ship."

"Then it's a good thing this isn't an MKX-7." Releasing her harness, she stood and moved to a reflective wall. Pressing her hand against it, a console emerged. "It's an MKX-10 prototype. Designed specifically to protect high-ranking government officials traveling in space. As my father is a Supreme Judge, and I do a great deal of interplanetary travel, I was allowed to test it."

"That's a military-grade defense system." Ranvir crossed the room, shocked at what he found. He reached around her and pressed a few buttons. "And it's fully loaded with torpedoes, missiles, shields, and a laser array system."

"As I said, we have a defense system," she told him smugly.

"Orders, Major?" Pike asked.

"We go back for Nas and his pod," Talyani said, looking at Pike as if that should have been obvious.

"We go to Tuater," Ranvir countered.

"What?!" Talyani rounded on him. "No! We have to rescue Nas and his pod."

"Do you know how many vessels are out there?" Ranvir pointed to the screen in front of Tane. "How are we supposed to know which one Demeter is in? Which ones contain members of his pod? Military ships are filling the area, searching for survivors. As soon as they find cyborgs among them, Shui will discover his plan has failed, and he'll order the pods destroyed."

Talyani's stunning blue eyes widened, and her bottom lip quivered. He hated being the cause, but heading to Tuater was logical. It's what Nas would do.

"Major, the Nissa and Prefect have arrived. They're powering up their weapons," Tane informed him.

"Shit." Ranvir was intimately familiar with both ships, having served on both. They were the most powerful battleships in the Kirs fleet. "Put it on the main screen."

As Tane did, two icons representing smaller ships suddenly disappeared.

"We can't just sit here and watch them be massacred!" Talyani exclaimed, looking at them in disbelief.

"We can't save them," Ranvir snapped.

"Maybe not, but we can at least give them a chance," she told him defiantly.

"And how do you suggest we do that?" Ranvir demanded.

"By firing on the ones firing on them."

Both Ranvir's brows shot up. "You want us to attack the Nissa and the Prefect?!"

"Not to destroy them because obviously we can't, but we can distract them. It'll give those in the pods time to get away."

"To where?" Ranvir couldn't believe they were even discussing this.

"I don't know." Her hands waved expressively. "But I know we have to give them a chance." Seeing only blank expressions on their faces, she pressed her hands together and pleaded. "Look, there are cyborgs in those escape pods and shuttles. They have to know they can alter their course like you did. They just need the chance. We can give it to them."

"She's right." Pike said, causing all eyes to turn toward him. "We know our cyborg brethren are attempting to reroute their pods, but that won't matter if they're destroyed first."

His gaze turned to Talyani. "Thanks to Mamsell Zulfiqar, we can assist them, which is what we all swore to do when we put on this uniform." He gestured to what the four of them were wearing. "To protect our people from any force that would destroy them. We started the rebellion in the first place to protect our people from Shui's unquenchable thirst for power. If we abandon them now, we're no better than him."

Ranvir didn't like what Pike was saying, but that didn't mean he wasn't right. Moving to stand behind the captain's chair, he began issuing orders. "Ganesha, let's see how fast this ship really is."

"Yes, sir." A slight smile on his face as he turned back to his console.

"Pike, get on the weapons console. Tane, keep me informed if more military ships arrive." Ranvir looked back to Wells. "You said you were a communications specialist?"

Wells stiffened in his seat. "Y...yes."

"Then get on the communications console," he ordered. "I want to know what's going on out there."

Wells slowly removed his harness, rose from his seat, and went to the one at the communications console.

"What about me?" Talyani asked, pulling Ranvir's gaze back toward her.

He pointed to the chair she'd sat in earlier, his expression forbidding. "Get your ass back in that chair and strap in. I can't be worried about you while we're making combat maneuvers."

Talyani's eyes widened, but she did what he said.

Ranvir couldn't believe he'd said that. Nas was the cyborg she'd come to save.

Nas was the one she'd risked her life for.

Not him.

He needed to remember that.

She wasn't his to worry about.

Chapter Four

Talyani was grateful she'd obeyed the major's orders as the Troubadour went through a series of maneuvers that, even strapped in, flung her first over one arm of her seat and then the other. Her cap flew off, causing all the curls she'd secured under it to explode.

She saw Vujcec was in the same predicament, while the cyborgs never lost their balance even though they were all standing, except for the one in the pilot's seat. How was that possible?

Looking forward, she realized the major had minimized the navigation screen to one corner of the main viewing screen, allowing him to see what was happening in front of the ship.

How he was able to bark out orders amidst the chaos calmly, she couldn't understand. Maybe it was part of becoming a cyborg. After his transition, Nas had become more distant, not that he'd been forthcoming before becoming a cyborg. He had been interested in her life, in making sure she wasn't being taken advantage of, and he made sure she knew if she were ever in trouble, he'd be there for her.

It was one of the reasons she'd known she had to do the same for him when she'd discovered the emperor's plans. The other reason was that she loved him.

Oh, she loved her mother and father, but that was different. They were all about power, prestige, and each other, in that order.

Having a child was a means to an end—something to be done for their social standing, like wearing the right dress to the right event. At least until she won Worlds, then they'd become proud doting parents, gushing about how they'd always known how talented she was. Nas was the only one who really cared about Talyani, the person, not the image. If she lost him, she wasn't sure what she'd do.

"Fire."

The major's order pulled her from her dark thoughts to watch streaks of white leave the Troubadour and turn into bright flashes.

"Direct strike on the Nissa," Pike announced.

"Damage?" Ranvir demanded.

"Minimal," Pike replied. "They raised their shields."

"Hard right!" Ranvir ordered when a burst of white headed towards them. Ganesha obeyed, and it flew right by them.

"That was a plasma burst," Pike informed everyone. "The Nissa isn't fucking around."

"Did you think they would?" Ranvir asked dryly. "Are they turning to follow us? Did our distraction work?"

"Yes," Tane told him, his gaze fixed on the navigation screen.

"And the Prefect?" Ranvir asked.

"Still firing on the escape vessels," Pike reported. "Although they've missed more than they've hit."

The major sat back in his chair. "Get their attention, Pike."

"Yes, Major."

Talyani watched as Pike sent multiple streams of white towards the battleship. The streams turned into several blinding explosions. Flinching, her hand flew up to cover her mouth in shock.

"What the fuck!" Pike cursed. "They didn't raise their shields."

"The Nissa is coming up behind us," Tane's emotionless voice filled the bridge. "They're firing."

Talyani's hands clenched the armrests of her seat, and sweat formed on her brows as she watched the streaks of white race toward them. Gods, was this the end?

"Raise rear shields," the major ordered. "Pike, head towards Tyurma. Let's see if we can lure the Nissa away."

"And the Prefect?" Tane asked.

"They're broadcasting that they are disabled," Wells told them, cupping his hand over his in-ear monitor. "They're requesting aid."

"It should take more than that to disable the Prefect." Pike's gaze shot to Ranvir's.

"Yes, it should have," Ranvir agreed, his gaze returning to Pike. "Tane, how many vessels have escaped?"

"All the shuttles have left the area in various directions, as have most escape pods. The rest are still on their auto heading. Back to Kirs."

Suddenly, Talyani slammed back into her seat. She cried out as the Troubadour shuddered.

Ranvir's head jerked in her direction. Something she couldn't define passed over his expression.

"That was a direct hit," Pike told Ranvir what he already knew. "Rear shields at fifty percent."

Ranvir nodded his understanding. "Then it's time to go. Ganesha, get us out of here. Max speed."

"Yes, Major."

"But," Talyani began, only to clamp her lips together at the sharp look the major sent her.

"Anyone wanting and able to get away has," he told her. "It's time we do the same."

∞ ∞ ∞ ∞ ∞

Talyani ran through the corridors of the Troubadour to her suite. She hadn't been able to stay on the bridge, not when she knew the people left behind were being murdered—knowing that Nas could be one of them.

Entering her bedroom, she threw herself onto her bed and began to sob. *'Oh, Gods. Had she done all this for nothing?'*

Risked her life.

Destroyed her career.

Only to lose Nas anyway?

"No." Pushing herself up, she wiped her face. She wouldn't accept that. "Nas isn't dead. He's too smart. He'd have gotten away. Now I just have to find him."

∞ ∞ ∞ ∞ ∞

Ranvir didn't react when Talyani ran from the bridge, even though his enhanced hearing caught her nearly silent sob. He didn't have time to deal with an emotional female. He needed to ensure the growing number of ships heading their way couldn't track them.

"Wells, what are you picking up?" he demanded.

"There's a lot of cross chatter, but Shui has released a statement claiming that instead of accepting the just and lawful punishment they'd received for treason, the rebels chose to overpower their guards and commit mass suicide, without regard for the innocent lives they were taking with them."

"He's blaming the Rebellion for the massacre," Ranvir huffed humorlessly.

"Which means he can't allow *any* survivors," Tane pointed out.

"He'll have all of us hunted down," Pike added.

"The Nissa is reporting that a ship with the designation of the Troubadour attacked it." Wells' announcement cut through the chatter and had every head turning toward him.

"Shit!" Ranvir swore. "I forgot to deactivate the transponder."

"I've got it." Wells fingers rapidly moved over the communications console.

"You know how to deactivate a transponder?" Ranvir's eyes narrowed into sharp slits.

"It's part of the communications array, isn't it?" Wells fired back, his fingers never slowing. "Done."

"That fast?" Ranvir's suspicion grew. Not even a cyborg could deactivate the high-security transponder that fast, and Wells wasn't one.

"I figured you wanted it done quickly, so I deactivated the entire outgoing communications array." Wells swung around in his chair to face Ranvir. "We'll be able to receive but not respond. I can reactivate communications once I have the time to isolate the transponder. You know the transponder must be active if we want to dock anywhere. Don't you?"

"Yes," Ranvir bit out, causing Wells to flinch and turn back to his console. "Tane, is the Nissa still tracking us?"

"No, Ganesha altered course as soon as the transponder was deactivated. The Nissa is still on our original course, but I doubt they will be for long. Admiral Siller isn't stupid. He's not going to try tracking a ghost."

Ranvir knew that, too. "What about the Prefect and the other ships?"

Tane scanned the massive amount of data before him. "The Prefect hasn't moved, but it isn't firing on the remaining pods. The other ships seem to be pursuing the escaping vessels."

"Any way we can assist them?" Ranvir asked and saw Pike raise an eyebrow. "Yes, I know our shields aren't one-hundred percent, but if they can't detect us, we may be able to assist at least some of our brethren. It will also allow us to try and connect with members of our pods. If we can, we can set up a rendezvous point."

"How?" Wells swung around to ask. "The communications array is down."

Ranvir ignored Wells' question and looked to Ganesha. "Set course for the closest group of vessels. Pike, be ready on weapons."

"Yes, Major," they both replied.

∞ ∞ ∞ ∞ ∞

Done with her pity party, Talyani rose and entered her closet. She wanted to get out of her borrowed clothes and into something that made her feel like her. She'd just entered the room when everything shuddered, and she fell against a wall.

"What the hell!" She tried to stand, but the room lurched sideways, flinging her into a corner. "Gods damn it!" she shouted at the bridge. "Can't you give a girl some warning?"

Pressing her back against a wall, she braced her feet on one of the secured cabinets. Grateful she had been when the ship tipped onto its side again. What the hell was that arrogant cyborg doing? She thought they were running away.

The Troubadour wasn't shuddering the way it had when they'd been under attack, and she couldn't hear any weapons fire, but that didn't mean anything. The ship had extensive soundproofing, especially in her quarters so that she wouldn't be disturbed. She regretted that now.

Finally, the ship seemed to stabilize. Rising, she quickly stripped off her clothes and pulled on a pair of pants and an oversized sweater. They were what she called her 'real' clothes. The ones she could be Taly in. They were the complete opposite of the professional ones that filled the majority of the closet. Those were all glitz and glamour that was Talyani, and while she enjoyed wearing them for interviews and on stage, they weren't practical for everyday life.

Moving to the opposite wall, she selected a pair of comfortable exercisers. Pulling them on, she exited the closet and crossed the bedroom to her private bathroom.

Inside, she got the first look at herself since that morning. Gods, she was a mess. The long silky curls she was known for were now a knotted nest. Sighing, she reached for a brush and began the arduous task of detangling the mass. As she did, the ramifications of everything that happened today hit, and she began to shake.

Dropping the brush, she gripped the edge of the counter.

Oh, Gods, she was a fugitive now.

She was a fugitive on a ship with four rebel cyborgs, none of which were her half-brother, and a fan who seemed to know how to handle a communications station. Could she trust any of them? The one with the major's insignia had immediately taken command after she'd freed them, and the other cyborgs had followed him, even though his first order had been to abandon the rest of their fellow cyborgs.

How long before he ordered them to do the same with her?

They had control of her ship. They didn't need her. Not even for her access code because, as cyborgs, they'd eventually crack it.

Then there was Vujcec Wells. Her 'fan' who'd so easily turned on her when the major had said *he* was of no use to them. No. She couldn't count on him either.

She could only rely on herself the same way she did on stage.

She took a deep breath, picked up the brush, and worked on her hair. She was Talyani Zulfiqar. She was more than a pretty face and a famous voice. Nas was always telling her that. Maybe she needed to start believing it. After all, she'd already done the impossible.

"Gods be damned!" she cursed as the brush got stuck in her hair. "I'm never going to get through this. I should just cut it off."

But she couldn't. Her fans would riot. They loved her hair. It stood out; no matter how people tried, they could never imitate its unique color or the large natural curls. It made her instantly recognizable, even without facial enhancements.

Her eyes widened at the realization.

It made her recognizable.

That wasn't a good thing for a fugitive.

Leaving the brush where it was stuck, she reached into a drawer and pulled out the scissors her hairstylist used to trim her ends. Taking a deep breath, she went to work.

Time to become who she really was.

Taly.

Chapter Five

Vujcec stumbled into the dining room in desperate need of food and some type of stimulant. He wasn't a cyborg. He couldn't go hour after hour without a break, especially not after everything that happened today. Reaching up, his hand paused before touching his still throbbing cheek.

Branded.

He was branded a traitor.

Gods, what was he going to do?

Where was he going to go?

Who could he trust?

Not those cyborgs. They'd been ready to leave him on the transport ship.

"There should be some burn cream in medical."

The softly spoken words had him spinning around, his gaze searching. "What?"

"There should be some burn cream in medical," Talyani repeated from where she sat across the room.

She had entered the dining room some time ago after her stomach reminded her she hadn't eaten since the day before. The Troubadour was fully stocked with a variety of foods. Most of it was in replicators. It was the easiest and safest way to prepare food in space. There were also fresh items, as Talyani always traveled with a private chef.

At least that's what her fans believed, but the truth was *she* liked to cook. It calmed her, which was why she'd been finishing a veggie omelet when Vujcec had walked in.

"Tal...Talyani?" he stuttered, his gaze traveling over the changes in her appearance.

She raised a hand to the short curls now framing her face. "Taly," she corrected.

"I didn't recognize you."

"That was the point." She gestured to a wall behind him. "The replicators are over there if you're looking for something to eat."

She watched Vujcec hurry to the first replicator and push buttons. He quickly returned with a full tray and sat down across from her.

At her raised eyebrow, he shrugged, a bright flush filling his cheeks. "They barely fed us after we were captured."

"Didn't want to waste the resources," she muttered. Shui planned to go to war. To do that, he needed resources. Resources that condemned people didn't need. It was one of the reasons she'd been so shocked Shui had been willing to sacrifice transport ships. Forgetting about that, she asked a more pertinent question. "Why were we flying so erratically earlier?"

Vujcec swallowed before answering. "We distracted the ships following the escaping pods since they can't track us."

"What do you mean they can't track us?" Taly was the first to admit she didn't know everything there was to know about her ship. But even she knew every ship could be tracked.

"I disabled the communications array, at least the outgoing portion." He shoveled in another mouthful and swallowed before continuing. "The transponder is a part of it. Now they can't track us."

"So the major did go back to help," she murmured absently.

"Don't think he did it out of the goodness of his heart," Vujcec sneered, continuing to eat. "If any of them even still have one. He did it to see if they could contact any of the members of their pods and set up a future rendezvous point."

"You claim to be a communications specialist working for the rebellion," she sneered at him, "but don't seem to know anything about them."

"I know enough," he fired back.

"Really? Yet you don't know how they can send transmissions when the communications array is down."

"And you do?" he challenged.

"Yes," she told him.

"What do you know?" a sharp voice demanded.

They both jerked in their seats and then looked toward the door. The major stood there glaring, the CR brand standing out in stark relief against his cheek.

Taly wasn't going to answer for a moment, then realized that was childish. "You have an NNP, neural net processor. It can be either an open or closed network. Nas told me about it once, saying how efficient communications were within a pod and that it saved his life more than once. You must be within a certain range to use it, which is why you wanted to get close to the escaping vessels."

His hard glare had her shrugging with a nonchalance she didn't feel. "So were any of you able to contact the other members in your pods?"

"What makes you think the four of us aren't a pod?" Ranvir demanded.

"Because if you were, you never would have discussed your plans in front of us." She gestured to Vujcec and herself.

Ranvir couldn't dispute that. Nas's lover was obviously more than a pretty face. "None of us were able to make contact," he finally told her.

"Crap," she cursed, sliding away from her unfinished meal, no longer hungry. "So what now?"

There was a long pause, but finally, he told her. "Now we head to Tuater."

"But..." Taly broke off when she saw him weave ever so slightly and questioned, "When was the last time you ate or reenergized?"

"I'm fine," the major snapped.

"You're not," Taly fired back. Standing, she crossed the room and opened a panel revealing several thick, slightly curved sticks.

"What are those?" Vujcec asked, having followed behind them.

"Power grips," Taly told Vujcec, but her gaze remained on the major. "This is the latest in reenergizing terminals. It's supposed to restore your energy levels instantly when you grip it."

"These aren't supposed to be available yet," he muttered, moving closer to inspect the devices.

"Again," she said dryly, "this is a prototype ship. It comes with lots of new things. There are several stations spread out across the ship."

Reaching out, Ranvir's hand encircled one of the power grips, and he stiffened. She watched his eyes close as his systems absorbed the onslaught of power. Nas had once told her that reenergizing was a long agonizing process. It started as a low burn and then finished as an inferno. In combat, the reenergizing was fast and burned like flowing lava.

She'd never seen the new power grips used and hoped they lived up to their billing. The recipient was supposed to feel only a slight tingle during the transfer.

When the major opened his eyes, he released the grip and stepped back. She was instantly at his side. "Are you all right?" she asked, carefully touching his arm.

Ranvir's intense brown gaze locked with hers before glancing down to where her hand rested on his bicep. She quickly let him go.

"I'm fine." He wasn't going to tell her, her touch had been more electrifying than the power grips.

"So they work?" she asked, looking from the grips back to him.

"Yes, my energy is now at its optimum level." He tilted his head to the side, gaze narrowing. "You cut your hair."

She subconsciously lifted a hand to her hair. "Yes. I figured I needed to change it so I wasn't recognizable."

"It won't help," he snapped.

"What? But..."

"It doesn't change how beautiful you are."

Taly wasn't sure who was more shocked at his statement, her or the major. She didn't think the gorgeous cyborg even liked her, let alone noticed her looks. Before she could say anything, he spun on his heel and left the room.

"Wow. I didn't think cyborgs were capable of that," Vujcec said, reminding her of his presence.

"Of what? Taly asked absently, her gaze on the door the major had gone through.

"Noticing beautiful things."

Taly rounded on him, her blue eyes flashing. "They're still human. They've just been enhanced. They have thoughts and feelings. They wouldn't have risen up against Shui if they didn't."

"Sorry. Sorry." Vujcec raised his hands in surrender. "I forgot you were involved with one."

"What are you talking about?" Her brows drew together. No matter what the media outlets claimed, she hadn't been involved with anyone in years.

"This Nas you risked your life to save," he reminded her. "You must really love him."

"Of course I do." She couldn't believe he would think she didn't. "He's my brother."

"What?!" Vujcec's eyes bugged out of his head. "How's that possible? You're the only child of a Supreme Judge. Your parents tried for years to have you. You're their miracle child." He spouted off the information given to her fans, but Taly ignored him. Instead, she rushed after the major.

∞ ∞ ∞ ∞ ∞

Ranvir stomped through the halls of the Troubadour. He couldn't believe he'd said that to Talyani even though it was true. Yes, she'd cut her hair, but it did nothing to lessen her beauty. Nothing ever could. He rubbed the spot over his heart. He didn't understand why she affected him, especially since she belonged to a male he greatly respected.

He needed to find Nas, and soon, before these feelings he had for Talyani grew.

"Major!" He stiffened, not wanting to acknowledge her. She was a temptation he didn't need. "Please, Major!"

Unable to ignore the plea in her voice, he spun around to face her. He masked his expression to make sure none of his inner conflicts showed on his face. "What?"

"I... I just want to thank you. For everything you've done." When he continued to stare silently, she sighed. "Look, it's obvious you don't like me, but if we're going to survive, we have to work together."

"I never said I didn't like you," he denied gruffly.

"You didn't have to," she huffed. "It's in every look you give me."

"And how do I look at you?" he asked, genuinely curious. He thought he'd successfully concealed his reaction to her.

"Like my very presence irritates you."

"It does," he admitted before he could stop himself.

He instantly regretted his words when her face paled, and she stepped backward. He hadn't meant to hurt her.

Now he understood why her fans adored her. She let them see everything she felt. Cyborgs weren't allowed to show their emotions. Would she be that open and responsive in bed?

"But why?" Her striking blue eyes searched his for the truth.

"Because you shouldn't be here," he growled. His anger grew, remembering the present danger. "You should be back on Kirs. Safe. You risked your life when you didn't need to. No male is worth your life, no matter how much you love him."

"Nas is," she told him firmly.

"Would he feel the same way?!" Ranvir demanded, moving forward until her back was pressed against the wall, caging her between his arms. Heat exploded between them. His body was close enough he could feel each breath she took. "How will he feel when he finds out what you've done? What you've risked?"

"He'll be pissed," she readily admitted as she defiantly glared at him, apparently not intimidated by his size. "But he'll also understand. You protect your family."

"Family?" He pulled back slightly, giving her a confused look.

"Yes, Nas is my brother, well, half-brother."

The computer part of Ranvir's brain quickly calculated this new information, pulling up his memories of Nas, of all the missions they'd been on together. They'd always conducted a debriefing within their team, above and beyond what the military demanded. Reiji, Nas's dad, had stated it made them a more efficient unit. They'd been in-depth and detailed, with each member giving a step-by-step account of their actions and why.

Except on the Giles mission after Reiji and Nas had separated from the team and secured the family of a Supreme Judge. On that mission, they'd been vague. He hadn't thought anything about it, assuming it was because of the family's status. Now, he realized it was because it'd been very personal to Nas and his father.

He remembered how much crap he'd given Nas for watching the Worlds competition that year. They'd been patrolling the outer edges of the Eridani Sector at the time and had just returned from back-to-back missions when the broadcast, delayed because of the distance, had finally come through. When Talyani had won, Nas reacted as if he had a personal stake in it. Now Ranvir realized he did. Talyani was his half-sister.

"How in the name of the Gods was that not discovered?" he all but shouted.

The government kept extensive records of all its citizens. It was how they managed to round up the family members of anyone involved in the rebellion.

"Because my father had the documentation altered before I was born," she told him, anger and disgust flashing across her face. "He couldn't be associated with someone from District Twelve, let alone have married one. Not if he wanted to be a Supreme Judge."

Ranvir was surprised at her vehement tone. "You don't believe D-Twelvers are beneath you?"

"No. Why would I? The only difference between them and me is where they were born."

He could tell she honestly believed that. How was that possible when she'd grown up the daughter of a Supreme Judge? Gods, she was incredible. And she wasn't Nas's. Before his processors could stop him, he leaned down and pressed his lips against hers.

∞ ∞ ∞ ∞ ∞

Momentarily stunned, Taly didn't immediately respond. When his tongue swept across her lips, she readily opened them. As their tongues tangled, she sank her fingers into his hair, surprised at how thick and silky the short strands were. Her legs wrapped around his hips when he lifted her off her feet, pressing her hot center against the bulge in his pants.

Gods, it felt so thick and hard. It had been so long since she'd been with anyone, and she wanted to be with.... Her entire body stiffened. Gods, she didn't even know his name.

The major felt her tense and lifted his head far enough to search her eyes. "What's wrong?"

"This... this isn't right."

"Why?" he growled. "Because I'm a cyborg?"

"What?" Her expressive eyebrows drew together in confusion before they shot up in shock. "No! Don't be stupid. It's because I don't know your *name*." She unwrapped her arms and legs from around him only to find herself still suspended. "Please let me down."

He slowly lowered her, never breaking eye contact, but he didn't step back. "It's Ranvir, Ranvir Somerled."

"I'm Talyani," she began, but he cut her off.

"I know who you are," he ground out.

"But I prefer Taly," she continued as if he hadn't interrupted.

"Major, sensors are picking up a long-range contact. A big one." Tane's voice came over the ship's comms system.

"We'll finish this later," Ranvir told her, then spun on his heel and walked away.

Chapter Six

"What have you got, Tane?" Ranvir demanded, entering the bridge.

"A deep-space convoy," the navigator told him.

"Any evidence they've detected us?" Ranvir questioned.

"No, even if our transponder were active, they don't have long-range scanning capabilities." Tane's eyes remained fixed on the screen before him.

"Let's keep our distance anyway," Ranvir ordered, looking to Ganesha, who nodded.

"I'm picking up some ship-to-ship chatter," Pike stated, having taken over the comms center when Wells left.

"About?" Ranvir demanded.

"What's happened over the last few days," Pike turned to address Ranvir. "Apparently, the emperor has placed a bounty on the head of every rebel turned in. Dead or alive. They're discussing what to do if they run into any."

"What's the consensus?" Taly asked, having followed Ranvir onto the bridge, not understanding the shocked stares until she remembered her hair.

"Mixed," Pike finally replied. "The only thing they agree on is that they never want to meet one."

"Major."

Ranvir pulled his gaze from Taly's kiss swollen lips. "What is it, Tane?"

"Sensors are detecting ships on an intercept course for the convoy, weapons hot," Tane announced.

"Pirates," Ranvir bit out as the ships appeared on the main screen.

"That would be my assessment," Tane agreed.

"Does the convoy have any defensive capabilities?" Ranvir looked to Pike.

"Not enough," Pike told him as a streak of white left one of the advancing ships, striking the last ship in the convoy.

Angry at the turn of events, Ranvir kept his gaze on the screen. "Status."

"The ship was able to raise its shields, but it took damage," Pike told them. "The second ship is preparing to fire."

"We have to help them," Taly told them, drawing their attention again.

"It's not our fight," Ranvir told her.

"Neither was helping the other rebels, but you did it because it was the right thing to do." Taly fired back. "This is no different. There are innocent people out there."

"Who will turn us in for credits the moment they get the chance," Ranvir argued back.

"Then we don't give them that chance," she told him. "But we can't just stand by and do nothing."

Ranvir's gaze locked with Taly's. He wouldn't hesitate to assist the convoy if he were with his pod. He knew those cyborgs, knew how they thought and how they reacted. These cyborgs, even though they followed his orders, were unknowns. Going into battle with unknowns was a sure way of ending up dead.

Then there was Talyani.

To risk her...

"Major, the second ship has fired," Tane announced.

Ranvir spun around in time to see the weapons strike the same ship.

"The ship's shields have failed. The pirates are maneuvering to board her," Tane reported flatly.

"The rest of the convoy?" Ranvir coolly asked.

"Leaving the area at max speed," Tane told him.

"They're abandoning them?" Taly's whispered voice filled with horror.

"They're sacrificing them," Ranvir corrected. "So the rest can survive. It's the most logical and strategic decision when there's no hope of victory."

"It's the coward's way," Taly spat, her hands fisting. "It's what Shui would do."

"She's right," Vujcec agreed, having returned to the bridge. "I did more on Kirs than forwarding messages between rebels. I managed to hack into palace communications before I was caught. Do you know how many innocents Shui sacrificed to lure out members of the rebellion?"

"Thousands, hundreds of thousands, and he did it not because it was logical and strategic, but because he *enjoyed* it. He enjoys hurting people just like he enjoyed doing this to us." He gestured to his cheek. "I know I'm not a cyborg or even military, but I damn well know that I never want to be like Shui. I vote we assist them."

"This isn't a democracy," Ranvir snarled.

"It isn't the military either," Vujcec refused to back down, "and in case you've forgotten, this ship isn't yours. It's Talyani's, so *she's* in charge. Not you."

Absolute silence filled the bridge. Everyone, including Taly, waited to see how Ranvir would respond to that challenge.

"He's right." Ganesha spun around in the pilot's chair. "We're no longer members of the military. We're fugitives. The rules we were forced to live by, the orders others forced us to follow, are no more. Now *we* make the rules, and I, for one, am tired of being told to stand down or stand by when I know we could make a difference. So, in this, I'm with Wells, but this ship is Mamsell Zulfiqar's, so the final decision is hers."

"Pike?" Ranvir looked to the weapons specialist.

"Assist."

Ranvir's gaze went to the navigator. "Tane?"

"Assist."

Ranvir turned to Taly. "What are your orders, Captain?"

Taly's eyes widened in shock. She held up her hands and waved them in the air. "Now, wait a minute. While I agree the ship is mine, I have absolutely no clue how to fly her, use her weapons, or fight pirates."

"Are you saying you wish me to take over command?" Ranvir asked stiffly.

Taly's gaze locked with his. "If you're willing to help that ship, then yes."

Ranvir spun on his heel with a nod and began snapping out orders. "Ganesha, get us there. Pike, power up the weapons. Vujcec, get on the comms. Tane, make sure there are only the convoy ships out there."

Ranvir guided Taly to the captain's chair as everyone moved to obey. He knelt down and secured the safety harness around her. "Sit and remain silent."

Rising, he stood beside her chair and faced the main screen. "Pike, status."

"Weapons hot. Targets acquired," came the instant answer.

Using his enhanced cybernetic brain to calculate the odds of every possible strike and the resulting damage, Ranvir assessed the battle's outcome. "Take out the farthest ship. Stagger the hits."

Although focused on the battle before him, Ranvir still noticed how Taly's fingers tightened on the arms of the chair as three white streaks shot out of the Troubadour. They arched over the convoy ship before descending sharply, striking the front of the farthest pirate ship one after the other. The ship exploded, its pieces blown away from the convoy ship as he'd planned instead of damaging it.

"What's the status of the remaining pirate ship?" Ranvir muttered.

"They attached to the convoy ship right before we attacked," Tane informed him.

"Shit," Ranvir cursed.

"Why's that bad?" Taly asked.

Ranvir glanced down at her. "The pirates know if we attack their ship now, it will destroy both ships."

"Oh." He could tell she hadn't realized that. "So what do we do?"

"*You* will do nothing but sit there." Ranvir's gaze traveled over the bridge. "Ganesha, position us to attach on the ship's opposite side. Pike, Tane, you're with me. We're going to clear that ship."

"With what?" Tane demanded, even as he rose from the navigation console. "We don't have any weapons."

"There are weapons in the security room." Ranvir's eyes shot back to her, and she continued. "I'm sure they're not what you're used to, but they're what my security used."

"Security?" Tane questioned, having come up to stand on the other side of her.

"Talyani can't travel without security," Vujcec spoke up. "She has rabid fans. Don't you guys know anything?"

Ranvir's gaze remained fixed on Taly, ignoring Wells. "Where's this room?"

"Right over there."

Taly pointed behind them to a door Ranvir hadn't had time to investigate. Striding over, he opened the door and entered the room. At first glance, it only contained a couch, several chairs, and a desk.

An array of weapons and communication devices lined the walls on closer examination, all secured behind dark glass. Opening the cabinets, he hummed his approval and began strapping on weapons. Whoever had stocked this arsenal hadn't been playing around. Returning to the bridge, he gestured to Pike and Tane.

"Arm up," he told Pike and Tane. "Ganesha, you'll remain onboard. Wells, bring the communications array back up. We'll need to communicate once we're aboard."

"But we'll be identifiable," Vujcec shrieked.

Ranvir ignored him as Pike and Tane returned loaded with weapons. "Let's go."

"Ranvir."

Turning, he found Talyani's eyes filled with concern. When was the last time someone outside his pod worried about his safety? It created the odd urge to reassure her.

"This is what we do," he told her shortly. "We're cyborgs. We'll be fine."

"I know, but... be careful." She looked at the other cyborgs. "All of you."

Giving her a nod, they left the bridge.

∞ ∞ ∞ ∞ ∞

Ranvir tapped the comms in his ear when they reached the hatch. "Ganesha."

"Achieving hard lock," Ranvir felt a slight bump, "now. Sensors show no one in your immediate area, but a group is heading in your direction. Unable to determine if they're hostile or friendly."

"Understood. Tane, open the hatch. Pike and I will cover you."

The young cyborg quickly followed the order. He pulled open the Troubadour's hatch, then, after a nod from Ranvir, pushed open the door on the other craft and immediately dropped into a defensive stance. It wasn't necessary, though. Ganesha had been right. There was no one there.

"Move out," Ranvir ordered.

"Incoming on your left," Ganesha spoke through their earpiece.

The three of them turned as one. Pirates advanced, weapons raised in their direction and fired.

∞ ∞ ∞ ∞ ∞

Taly bit her lower lip as she listened to the comms Vujcec put on speaker for them. Shouts and blaster fire poured through. Removing her harness, she leaped to her feet and pressed a hand to her stomach. The sound nauseated her in a way she hadn't been since she'd performed at Worlds.

Gods, if anything happened to Ranvir because she'd insisted on helping the other ship, she'd never forgive herself.

Nas always told her she was too soft-hearted, especially when she told him about some special appearances she made for 'ill' fans. He'd doubted many were actually ill, especially when one of them posted what was supposed to be a private visit all over his social media. After that, she was bombarded with requests, most of which she was forced to decline.

"Shit," Vujcec swore, his fingers flying over his console.

"What is it?" Ganesha demanded.

"The captain of that ship is broadcasting that he's under attack. By cyborgs."

"What?!" Taly gave Vujcec a disbelieving look. "He can't possibly know you guys are on board."

"He's doing it because he hopes it will draw the attention of the military, and they'll come to their aid. Jam their transmission." Ganesha moved to stand next to Vujcec after he gave the order.

"All right, but it will take some time."

Ganesha pressed a button to activate the comms. "Major, be aware there may be hostiles among the ship's occupants. The captain is transmitting they are under attack by cyborgs."

"Understood," Ranvir replied.

"Vujcec, can you connect us with the other ship's bridge? Visual and audio?" Ganesha asked.

Looking confused, he said, "Yes, but why?"

"Just do it and take our guys off the speaker." He turned to Taly. "You're going to talk to them."

"What? Me? Why me?" Taly couldn't have been more shocked than if he'd demanded she start singing.

"Because you're the only one *not* branded," he pointed to the CR on his cheek. "If they know there really *are* cyborgs on their ship, they'll panic."

"Shit!" That made sense, but what was she supposed to *say*?

He must have understood her confusion. "Just tell them we're here to assist and get them to stop broadcasting the message before the military shows up."

Taking a deep breath, Taly moved back to the captain's chair and sat down, her shoulders back and chin tipped in a classic pose she used on stage. She could do this. She was Gods damn Talyani. She'd stood confidently before millions. She could handle sitting before a cargo ship captain.

With a nod to Vujcec, the other bridge appeared on the main screen. It was utter chaos. Shouts, weapons fire, and shrill orders were tossed out.

"This is Captain..." she fumbled for a name. She knew she couldn't use her real one, then nearly smiled when she knew which one to use. Luckily no one on the other bridge noticed. "Somerled. Reaching out to the captain of the ship currently under attack by pirates."

A short, fat man appeared on their screen, sweat running down his face as he spun around from the door he'd been helping barricade.

"Thank the Gods! This is Captain Ju of the transport ship, Celerity. We need your immediate assistance, Captain. We're being attacked."

She nodded sagely. "Yes, I can see. By *pirates*. We're here to assist you unless you prefer we don't."

"What?" His eyes rolled crazily. "Why would I not want that? We're a merchant vessel transporting merchandise and colonists to Gamma-2. We're not equipped to repel pirates."

She paused at his admission. "Then why are you transmitting that cyborgs are attacking you?"

He tugged at the collar of his shirt. "Well, it got your attention, didn't it?"

Holding back a sharp retort, she said, "You will immediately cease broadcasting erroneous information, or we'll leave you to your fate."

Ju looked to his left, then moved his finger across his neck to someone she couldn't see.

"They've stopped," Vujcec whispered. "The major says they've reached the bridge."

Taly gave a slight nod. "Our people are outside your door, Captain Ju. Let them in."

"What?" Ju frantically looked from her to the barricaded door. "Are you sure?"

"Yes. Now open the door," she ordered.

Chapter Seven

Ranvir kept his blaster up as they waited for the doors of the bridge to open. Vujcec had taken them off the speaker, but he'd kept the line open. So they heard everything happening on the Troubadour's bridge.

Logically, he understood why Ganesha had used Talyani, but that didn't mean he liked it. When he got back on the Troubadour, he'd make sure Talyani never exposed herself like that again. This captain had already shown he couldn't be trusted by abandoning the colonists he'd agreed to transport.

She may have cut her hair, but she was still easily recognizable. If this captain noticed and revealed she willingly traveled with rebels, she'd be hunted for the rest of her life, just like them, brand or no brand.

Ranvir found himself face-to-face with a muscular, blue-skinned male holding a blaster as the doors slid open. He didn't match the image he had from the captain's voice.

"Fuck!" Someone swore deeper in the room. "It really is cyborgs."

Ranvir ignored the comment, keeping his gaze locked with the Madae male holding the blaster. "You're the captain?"

"No," he said in a deep voice. "I'm Ree."

"I'm Captain Ju."

Ranvir tracked the whiny voice he recognized to an overweight, sweaty, red-faced male hiding behind the captain's chair. "What is the status of your ship?"

"St...status?" the captain stuttered.

"Yes, status. Are your engines operable? Life support? How many people are on board?" Ranvir fired off his questions. Questions any good captain would be able to answer.

"I... I don't know about the engines. We lost contact with engineering. Life support is holding for now. We have fifty colonists and five crew on board."

"And where are they?"

The captain swiped the back of his shaking hand over his brow. "What?"

"Where are the colonists?" Ranvir gritted out.

"How would I know?" Ju spat out. "They scattered as soon as we came under fire."

"Ganesha?" Ranvir spoke quietly, knowing the other cyborg would hear him.

"Scanning now, Major," Ganesha responded and, after a moment, continued. "The majority of them seem to be in the cargo bay. There's a group heading that way, but they're stopping to search rooms on their way."

"More pirates," Ranvir acknowledged. "How many?"

"Six, Major."

Ranvir looked to Ree. "Can you use that blaster?"

"Yes."

Ranvir nodded. "Guide us to the cargo bay."

"No!" Ju shouted as he moved to grab Ree's arm. "Ree has to stay here and protect me. I mean us." Ju gestured to the other crew member huddled on the bridge.

Ree shrugged him off with a glare. "I signed onto this ship to transport those colonists safely to Gamma-2, which means protecting them from pirates." His gaze returned to Ranvir. "We need to go left."

Ranvir kept a close eye on Ree as they made their way through the ship. The Madae were known as protectors but rarely traveled off their homeworld, a tiny planet on the other side of the Eridani Sector. For Ree to be this far from home was suspicious.

"I don't care! I want that fucking door opened!" an angry voice shouted.

Ranvir stepped in front of Ree, taking the lead and adjusting his blaster's aim.

"The cargo bay doors are to your right," Ree informed them quietly.

Ranvir pressed his back against the wall, then quickly looked around the corner, his cybernetic vision needing only an instant to take in everything before he pulled back. "Six targets. All armed with blasters. Pike, Tane, you take high. Ree and I will go low. Ready?" Receiving nods from all three, he gave the order. "Go!"

Focused on opening the cargo door, the pirates didn't notice them at first. Before they did, they were all on the ground. Dead.

"Contact the colonists," Ranvir ordered Ree. "Tell them it's safe to open the door."

Ree went to the open comms panel just outside the cargo bay door. Apparently, the pirates had been taunting the colonists through it.

"This is Ree. It's safe to open the door now. The pirates are dead."

After a moment, he got a response.

"How can we be sure you're telling the truth? That this isn't a trick?"

"You know me," Ree told them. "I wouldn't lie to you."

"Major," Ganesha's voice filled his ear.

Ranvir touched his earpiece. "What is it?"

"I'm getting dangerous readings from the Celerity's engines. They're approaching critical mass."

Ranvir muttered a curse under his breath. "How much time?"

"Ten minutes. Fifteen if we're lucky."

They had no time to waste. Ranvir raced to the comm panel, shoving Ree aside. "This is Major Somerled. The pirate's attack has damaged your ship's engines. They will reach critical mass in less than ten minutes. If you don't want to die, you will open this door. Now!"

He banged his fist on the door for emphasis. It took longer than Ranvir liked, but the door finally opened, and fifty scared faces of various ages and sexes stared back at him.

"Let's go," Ranvir ordered. "Pike, take point. Get us back to our ship."

The next few minutes were chaos. Ranvir had never understood the phrase 'like herding kassids,' but he did now. The colonists kept trying to break off so they could retrieve something they 'just couldn't live without.'

Didn't they understand that if they didn't get off this ship, they wouldn't live? As another male rushed into a room, Ranvir announced. "We will not be waiting for anyone who leaves this group!"

They finally reached the hatch leading to the Troubadour. Pike ushered the colonists through as fast as they could move. Shouts sounded from Ranvir's left. Spinning around, he raised his blaster only to lower it again when he saw Captain Ju and the remaining crew members hurrying in their direction.

"You were going to leave us!" Ju accused.

"I gave you as much consideration as you gave these colonists when you barricaded yourself on the bridge and left them to fend for themselves."

∞ ∞ ∞ ∞ ∞

Taly's fingers twisted together as they monitored Ranvir's and the colonists' progress through the other ship. Her gaze went from their dots on the main screen to the increasing temperature of the Celerity's engines, which Ganesha had enlarged on another screen to keep track.

They were running out of time. Taly rose from her seat as the dots neared where the Troubadour was attached. She couldn't take it anymore. "I'm going to help at the hatch."

Ganesha glanced at her over his shoulder. "What do you think you can do?"

Giving him a hard look, Taly bit out. "I can guide the colonists to the concert hall. There'll be enough seating for them, and the seats have harnesses. That will free up Ranvir, Pike, and Tane to help you get us out of here before the Celerity blows."

Not waiting for his response, she stormed off the bridge.

Ganesha looked to Vujcec. "Concert hall?"

"It's used to give private concerts for high-ranking officials." Vujcec frowned. "Are you that ignorant about who she is? Her life has been all over the news feeds for years. She makes a fortune giving those private performances."

"I'm a cyborg. I don't download *entertainment* feeds," Ganesha snarled.

"Then I feel sorry for you. If becoming a cyborg mutes your emotions, and you can't appreciate beauty and music, especially Talyani's music, the universe must be a very cold place for you."

Ganesha didn't reply, only turned around in the pilot's seat to prepare to disconnect from the Celerity. Looking at the main screen, he contacted Ranvir.

"Five minutes, Major."

"Understood, we're getting the last of them in now. Get us out of here as soon as you verify the hatch is sealed."

∞ ∞ ∞ ∞ ∞

Ganesha assuming she was useless bothered Taly. Yes, he'd supported that she was technically captain of the Troubadour, but she realized it was only because it was logical. Cyborgs were nothing if not logical. She'd gleaned that from her conversations with Nas, especially after he became a cyborg.

She'd forgotten that with her interactions with Ranvir. With him, she sensed more than a logical cyborg. At least she hoped so because she was beginning to care a great deal for him. Rounding the corner, she ran into a mass of crying people huddled together.

"No! You can't seal the hatch yet! My husband is still on the ship!" one woman cried out.

"He should have stayed with the group," Ranvir told her coldly.

"He went to get our credits!" The woman told him, clenching a baby tightly to her chest. "How can we start a new life with no credits?"

"You'll have to find out as your husband has abandoned you." Ranvir's attention went to his men. "Pike. Tane. Get to the bridge."

Taly was stunned at how cold and callous Ranvir appeared. Didn't he understand this young female's fear? She was a female alone in space—a female with a child. The odds of either of them surviving were slim to none without credits. Taly wanted to reassure her, but right now, she needed to get these people somewhere safe.

Walking up to the crying female, she put a comforting arm around her. "Let's get you and your baby somewhere more comfortable." She looked to the rest of the group. "All of you. We need to distance ourselves from your ship before it explodes."

Taly kept her arm around the young woman as she led the group to the largest room on the ship. The concert hall. It was where she refined her craft en route to performances. It was also where she gave private performances for dignitaries, something her father had insisted.

Taly fought him at first, but she changed her mind when she'd learned the obscene number of credits they were willing to pay. She knew some would see that as wrong, but those credits allowed her to lower the admission price for her public concerts, allowing everyone to attend.

"Why don't you sit here," she encouraged, leading the woman to one of the plush oversized viewing chairs, "and I'll help you strap in."

Pushing a button on the chair's arm, a harness wrapped in kani fur appeared.

"Why do we need to be strapped in?" the female sobbed.

"It's just a precaution. We'll have to ride out the shock wave if we're not far enough away from your ship when it explodes." She looked to the others who had followed them into the room. "Everyone. Find a seat and strap in. The harness release is on the chair's right arm."

Taly quickly moved around the room, helping people settle, and saw that a large, blue-skinned male was doing the same. No one else would notice the difference, but she recognized the slight vibration signaling it was picking up speed. She was nearly finished when the ship began violently rolling from side to side.

She grabbed for the arm of the closest chair but missed and flew across the aisle. Her back slammed into a wall. Crying out, she tried to regain her balance, but another roll of the ship tipped her forward. Her hip banged into the side of a chair. She fell, and her face butted against one of the supports.

Stunned, she still managed to wrap her arms around a support before her body was lifted off the floor and slammed back down onto it, knocking the breath out of her. Closing her eyes, she tightened her grip on the support and prayed it would be over soon.

Chapter Eight

Ranvir registered Taly's disapproval of his interaction with the colonist but couldn't let it affect him. They would all be dead. *She* would be dead if they didn't get some distance between them and the crippled Celerity. Pulling on the hatch, his cybernetic hearing picked up a faint cry.

"Wait! Please!"

Opening the hatch slightly, he saw a man less than fifty feet away running for his life toward him. The logical thing would be to seal the hatch and the man's fate. In the past, it's what he was ordered to do on more than one occasion.

But as Ganesha had said, they were no longer part of the military. They could no longer be ordered to stand down and stand by. Now it was up to them to make the right decisions.

Could he let that man die knowing he could save him? His cybernetic brain said yes. What was left of his human one said no. He followed his human one and opened the hatch further.

In seconds, the man was near enough for Ranvir to grab his arm and yank him into the Troubadour before quickly sealing the hatch. He couldn't save anyone else, but at least he'd saved one.

"Thank you! Thank you!" the man gasped between breaths. "I thought I was a goner."

Ranvir didn't reply, just spun on his heel and headed for the bridge.

"Wait! Where am I supposed to go? Where's everyone else? Where's my family?"

Ranvir didn't slow down and didn't bother to answer the man's questions. He needed to get to the bridge so he could assess the situation. He'd felt the Troubadour disconnect from the Celerity as soon as the hatch sealed. Now, by his calculations, they were accelerating at an extreme rate.

Crossing the doorway, he charged onto the bridge and demanded, "Status."

"Communications array shut down. Engines on the Celerity have reached critical mass," Ganesha told him calmly even as his fingers flew over the piloting console in front of him. "We won't be out of range for the worst of the shock wave. If we're lucky, anyone registering our transponder code will think we were destroyed with the Celerity."

"Raise the shields," Ranvir ordered.

"Shouldn't we..." Vujcec broke off when the ship began to shake. He barely had time to tighten his harness before the shock wave hit, flinging him back in his seat.

Ranvir spread his legs and gripped the back of the captain's chair to maintain his balance. The ship rocked hard to the left and then the right. The male colonist who'd followed him onto the bridge wasn't so lucky and rolled across the deck. Pike reached out and grabbed one of the colonist's arms to stop his dangerous fall. Ganesha piloted the ship through the shock wave until it finally passed, then stabilized the ship.

"Damage report," Ranvir demanded.

"Minor," Tane reported, his fingers rapidly moving over his consol. "The shields deflected the worst of it, but the power crystals for the rear shields are now down to ten percent. They're going to need to be replaced."

"Any contacts on navigation?" Ranvir demanded, looking at Tane.

"No," Tane told him.

"Where's my family?" the colonist demanded as he rose to his feet and shook off Pike's hold.

"Taly took them to the concert hall," Vujcec told him.

"Where's that?" The colonist looked to Vujcec.

"I'll show you." Vujcec unstrapped himself and gestured for the man to follow him.

Ganesha waited until the door closed before looking at Ranvir. "What took you so long sealing the hatch?"

"That man was lagging behind," Ranvir told him coolly. "I chose to wait for him."

"Putting us at risk," Ganesha growled.

"*We* make the rules now, isn't that right? Instead of being told to stand down or stand by," Ranvir shot Ganesha's words back to him. "I chose not to sacrifice a man's life when I didn't need to."

∞ ∞ ∞ ∞ ∞

Once the ship stabilized, the screams that had echoed off the concert hall's walls faded. Rolling onto her back, Taly tried to calm her breathing as she reached up and gingerly touched her cheek. While it was tender, her fingers didn't come back bloody, so she'd count that as a win.

She'd barely gotten to her feet before the Celerity's captain was in her face.

"You lied to me, *Captain Somerled*," he snarled.

"Did I?"

"You know you did." Ju was nearly foaming at the mouth. "You're traveling with *rebel cyborgs*! If I'd known that, I would never have allowed you on my ship!"

"Then you would be dead." Taly raised her voice, so everyone heard her. "You would all be dead! And for the record, you didn't let us on your ship. You didn't even know we were on board until I contacted you because you had barricaded your sorry, fat ass on the bridge. Leaving all the people you were supposed to be protecting to fend for themselves!"

His gaze rapidly traveled around the room, and he tried to defend himself. "I was sending out a distress call!"

"Which no one responded to, not even the ships from your own convoy." She wouldn't let this piece of shit wiggle out of what he'd done. "Also, for your information, I *am* the captain of this ship."

With that, she turned her attention to the rest of the room. "Is everyone okay? Is anyone hurt?" She moved to help people with their harnesses.

"What was that?" someone asked.

"Your ship exploding." She knew there was no way she could soften that blow.

"What?!" A large male shouted as he surged to his feet to glare at her. "No! Our supplies! Our equipment was on that ship."

"I'm sorry," was all she could say.

"Captain Ju's right," the same large male claimed. "This is those damn cyborgs' fault! The entire Kirs military is hunting them, but they stop to help us? Why? I'll tell you why," he continued before anyone could answer, "Because now everyone thinks we're dead and they can do whatever they want with us. Kill our children. Rape our women. Sell us all into slavery, and there's no one to stop them."

"Calm down, Feo," the muscular blue-skinned male put a hand on the other's arm only to have Feo shake it off.

"Don't tell me to calm down, Ree! I know what I know."

Taly couldn't believe anyone in the room was listening to this blowhard, but a low rumble of agreement began filling the room. Feeling their growing discontent and fear, she moved onto the stage and took control of the crowd the way she always did.

"That's enough!" She didn't need the sound system for her voice to bounce off the walls. The crowd quieted as it always did when she took the stage. "None of you actually believe that crap, do you?"

"Those males are cyborgs!" someone shouted.

"Yes, yes they are." She didn't bother to deny it. "They swore to protect the citizens of Kirs wherever they are. Which is exactly what they did by coming to your aid."

"They're traitors!" shouted another.

"If they were, would they put themselves at risk coming to help?" Taly demanded. "Those *pirates* would have killed your children. Those *pirates* would have raped your women. And it's those *pirates* who would have sold those who survived into slavery. Not these *cyborgs*."

When the concert hall door slammed open, everyone jumped and spun around in fear. Taly saw Vujcec walk in, followed by another male.

"Oved!" the female with the baby Taly'd helped screeched and pushed her way through the crowd.

"Sato!" The man rushed to the woman and baby, pulling them into his arms. "Are you all right?" He pulled back to look down at their daughter. "Is Uki?"

"We're fine," she reassured him, then pulled back to thump a fist on his chest. "Gods, Oved! What were you thinking? If Uki and I lost you..." she broke off and sobbed.

"I'm sorry, Sato," he murmured into her hair, pulling his family even closer. "It was stupid of me. No amount of credits is worth the risk of losing you and Uki. If that cyborg hadn't waited for me, I would have."

"We owe him everything then." She drew in a shaky breath.

"We do," he agreed.

"We all do," Ree's deep voice filled the room, and Taly felt the mood shift.

Leaving the stage, she moved towards Vujcec. "How are things on the bridge?"

"Good. What the hell happened to you?" he demanded, reaching out to touch the darkening bruise on her cheek.

Taly quickly pulled back. "I wasn't strapped in when the shockwave hit."

"What?" His hand fisted as he lowered it. "Fuck! I tried to tell Ranvir he needed to warn you. But everything happened so fast. Are you hurt anywhere else?"

Just her hip and back, but she wouldn't tell him that. "I'm fine, but some of the colonists got banged up. I want to take them to medical."

"Medical? The Troubadour has one?" The look Talyani sent his way had him huffing softly. "Of course it does."

∞ ∞ ∞ ∞ ∞

Vujcec came to an abrupt halt when he entered the room Talyani had led him and the colonists claiming to be injured. It wasn't a small room with the standard auto repair bed like he'd assumed. It was a complete medical suite with multiple high-tech beds and what looked like a full lab.

"You know how to use all of this?" He gestured around the room.

"Umm, well, actually no." She gave him a hopeful look. "Do you?"

"No, and you're not going to find any medical personnel among these colonists," he claimed.

"Why do you say that?" Taly's brows drew together.

"Because the last ship in a convoy carries those who pay the lowest fares," Vujcec explained. "It's why none of the other ships turned around to assist them. They're considered expendable. Medical personnel aren't."

Taly couldn't believe it. "*That's* why they didn't turn around?"

"Yes," Ree answered, having helped one of the colonists to medical. "It's also why the pirates targeted our ship. They knew we were the most vulnerable."

"That's not right," she argued.

"Life rarely is," Ree told her.

"How did you ever expect this to get used?" Vujcec asked, pulling Taly's attention back to the subject at hand.

"I have... had a medic who traveled with me. He knew how to use everything. Na..." she caught herself, looking at Ree. She wasn't going to reveal to him she'd planned on turning the Troubadour over to her half-brother. "It's my understanding cyborgs know how to operate it."

Vujcec went to the comm on the wall and touched the icon for the bridge. "Major Somerled, you're needed in medical."

It only took a moment for Ranvir to reply. "What's wrong? Is Taly hurt?"

Taly's breath caught at his instant question.

"I'm fine," Taly reassured him. "But several of the colonists need treatment, and neither Vujcec nor I know how to operate a med bed, and I was told you might."

"I'll be there momentarily."

∞ ∞ ∞ ∞ ∞

"Where's medical?" Ranvir demanded, looking to Tane.

"One deck down. Third door on the right." Tane quickly informed the major.

"Contact me immediately if any ships appear on the screen."

"Yes, Major," Tane responded.

Ranvir moved quickly through the ship, his heart pounding faster than it should. He couldn't get it to slow. With his cybernetics, that should be impossible. Taly had said she was fine, but he wouldn't regain control until he saw her with his own eyes. Reaching medical, he entered and stopped short. There were at least twenty colonists in the room.

"Taly! Where are you?" he demanded, scanning over the unfamiliar faces.

"I'm over here, Ranvir."

Turning, he found her kneeling a few feet away, speaking softly to a young girl cradling her arm. After a moment, she stood and faced him. His heart stuttered at the sight of the dark bruise on her cheek.

"You said you weren't hurt," he accused, rushing to her side. He gently probed the injury, watching each time she winced. A visual scan assured she would be fine. Relief left him trembling, and he dropped his hand to his side to hide it.

"I didn't say that. I said I was fine. Which I am. This," she gestured to her face, "is just a bruise. It'll heal. Especially if you know how to operate the med beds."

"The med..." he turned to where she'd pointed. Shock held him immobile. While med beds were standard on private high-end ships, there was never more than one, and they weren't the latest combat models capable of repairing a cyborg's metal framework. This one even appeared able to replenish nanobots if necessary.

Taly shouldn't own one, let alone two, but in the short time he'd known her, he'd discovered what was impossible for most was normal for Taly.

"So, do you know how to operate them?" Taly asked.

Ranvir moved to the control panel at the head of one of the beds. The computer in his brain quickly analyzed its make and model. "Yes. Once it scans the patient, you approve the treatment selected, and then the bed takes over."

"It's really that simple?" Her eyes widened in surprise.

"Yes."

"Show me," she demanded.

"Get on the bed," he ordered.

She rolled her eyes at him. "Not me. Sasha."

Before Ranvir could question who Sasha was, Taly lifted the child she'd been talking with onto the bed.

"Momma," the child cried out.

"It's okay, Sasha," her mother, nervously standing by, reassured her. "It won't hurt. I promise."

"She's never used a med bed before?" Taly asked, unable to keep the shock out of her voice. Med beds were used to give children immunizations and treat childhood illnesses.

"There was only one bed for our section of District Twelve," the woman replied defensively, "unless you are on the verge of dying, the Section Medic won't allow you access."

Ranvir could tell Taly wanted to rant and rave at how wrong that was, and he agreed. Every citizen should have the same access to health care, but he also knew that wasn't the case. Taly had only ever experienced the privilege of growing up as the daughter of a Supreme Judge and then the winner of the Worlds competition. He could tell she hadn't realized just how privileged she'd been until now.

She forced a bright smile on her face and focused on Sasha. "Hey, sweetie, so what will happen is you will lie back on this soft bed." She patted the med bed, showing Sasha it was soft. Then she helped the child lie back, still gingerly holding her arm across her chest. "Now, in a minute, the bed will activate, and it will feel like a weighted blanket is covering you, even though you won't be able to see it."

"I won't be able to move?" Frightened little eyes locked with Taly's.

"You can, but it would be better if you don't. If you're brave for just a few minutes, we can fix your arm, and it won't hurt anymore. Can you do that?"

"Momma?" Sasha's lower lip trembled as she looked at her mother.

Her mother moved closer so Sasha could see her. "You can do this, Sasha, and I'll be right here. You'll be able to see me the whole time."

It took a moment, but Sasha's lip stopped trembling. She looked to Taly and nodded.

Taly gave Sasha's good arm a reassuring squeeze, then went to where Ranvir stood behind the transparent partition separating the control panel from the bed.

"All right, show me what to do," she told him. "Vujcec, come over here and watch, too. The more of us who know how to use this, the better it will be."

As Vujcec approached, Ranvir shifted Taly, so her back was pressed against his front, preventing Vujcec from touching her.

"This is where you power up the bed," he told her, making sure his arm brushed hers as he moved to press a green icon on the dark panel. The console immediately lit up, followed by a soft hum. "Then you press this."

He felt Taly's breath catch and saw her nipples pebble beneath her shirt as he brushed his arm along the curve of her breast when he reached to touch the icon that read 'Diagnose.'

"Then you wait for the readout," he told her quietly.

Ranvir knew he shouldn't be touching Taly like this. The cybernetic part of his brain kept telling him to stop, but his human side kept overriding it.

Taly was hurt, and it had his protective instincts rising. They'd been bad enough when he thought she belonged to Nas. Now that he knew she was his sister, they were entirely out of control, especially after kissing her, something he wanted to do again. Tipping his head down slightly, he inhaled her unique scent, filing it away in his memory banks.

A beep from the console pulled his thoughts back to the task at hand. Straightening, he read the list of what the bed had discovered, arranged from most life-threatening to least, and heard Taly's shocked breath. For a child this size, the list was longer than he expected. Still, it was the arm they needed to repair right now.

"You then select what you wish done," he told her, touching only where the bone fracture in Sasha's arm was listed. "Then press initiate."

Before he could do that, Taly's hand stopped him. Frowning, he looked down at her.

"Why aren't you selecting everything?" she asked quietly, her gaze still fixed on the list of things the scan had discovered.

Malnutrition. Lung congestion from the dust all D-Twelvers had to deal with. Skin irritations from the same dust. At the top of the list was the detection of the presence of the Onkex virus, a devastating disease that would grow and kill Sasha within the next few years if left untreated.

"The fracture is the immediate concern," he replied just as quietly.

"But the rest needs treating, too," she hissed.

"It will take more time and use resources we may need later."

"She's a child." She glared up at him. "She deserves every chance we can give her. The resources can be replaced."

"It will take more time," he warned her.

"How much more?" she demanded.

Ranvir quickly calculated the time difference. "Five minutes. So a total of seven."

He wasn't surprised at how Taly's eyes flared with anger or when she slid her finger down the list, selecting every item before pressing initiate.

"Is there something wrong?" Sasha's mother asked, concern filling her eyes as she looked from Ranvir to Taly.

Taly gave her a reassuring smile. "No. I was asking Major Somerled how long he thought the bed would take."

"And how long is that?" the mother asked.

"Seven minutes. In seven minutes, your daughter will be completely healed. Can you hold out that long, Sasha?" Taly spoke louder so the little girl who had tilted her head back could hear her. "You can talk if you want."

"I can do that," Sasha told her.

"Good." Taly looked back to Ranvir. "Does the other bed work like this one?"

"Yes."

She turned to Vujcec. "You saw how to run the bed?"

"Yes, and yes, I'll handle it as you did," letting her know he agreed to ensure all the colonists' ailments were treated.

"Good," she nodded.

"The readout for the remaining treatment time is here." Ranvir gestured to a decreasing number in the upper right-hand corner of the console as Vujcec moved to the other bed.

"Got it."

Nearly two hours later, the last of the colonists who had come to medical had been treated and were on their way back to the concert hall.

"Now you," Ranvir growled, lifting Taly onto a med bed.

"I told you I was fine," she argued even as she swung her feet up and lay back.

"Which is why you have a black eye." Moving to the control console, he shoved Vujcec away from it and began the scan. When it came to Taly, he trusted no one but himself. She was his.

When the results came back, he glared at Taly. His lips pressed into a firm line, and it took a moment before he could speak. "You said you were fine! You have a fractured cheekbone! Not to mention multiple contusions, including a large one on your hip." He checked the treatments listed and initiated the process, unable to believe he'd allowed anyone else to be treated first. He should have forced her onto the bed.

"If that's all after being thrown around the concert hall like a rag doll, then I'll take it," she murmured.

"What do you mean 'being thrown around?'" he demanded.

"She didn't have time to strap in before the shockwave hit." Vujcec gave him an accusing look. "I tried to tell you we needed to warn them."

"Stop it, you two," Taly chastised. "It's my fault. I wasn't strapped in, and I'm sure Ranvir would have informed us if there'd been time. Now, how much longer?" She could tell the treatment was working because her headache was rapidly fading.

"Two more minutes," Ranvir bit out.

Closing her eyes, she waited.

Chapter Nine

Ranvir didn't want to leave Taly's side. After the med bed finished, she insisted on returning to the concert hall to guide the colonists to the dining hall.

Now she leaned forward, instructing them on how to use the replicators. The position drew her pants taut against her bottom. His gaze dropped accordingly, and his lust stirred. He hadn't had to deal with those sensations since his cyborg conversion.

Her brows creased in concentration as a woman pointed to an item, and Taly answered. Her lips curved in response to another comment, and her smile tugged at Ranvir's heart.

"Major, you're needed on the bridge," came over Ranvir's earbud.

Ganesha's reminder made him realize he'd never allowed the others to recharge. Their energy levels had to be running critically low, yet they'd said nothing. Walking over to Taly, he gently pulled her to the side.

"I'm needed on the bridge. Where are the closest power grips to that area?"

Taly's eyes widened, and he could tell she'd just realized the same thing he had. "There's a set right next to the weapons console. Just push on the panel as I did here."

Nodding, he reached up to lightly caress the cheek where the bruise had been. "I'll be back as soon as I can."

"Take your time." She leaned into his touch. "After everyone's done eating, I will get them settled in their rooms."

"Rooms?" he asked.

"Yes, there are twenty on this deck for the crew and five suites on the main deck plus the captain's quarters. Once I'm done here, I'll come up and show you. I know cyborgs can last for a long time, but even recharged, you need to sleep."

"We're capable of going several days without it," he told her, his voice deepening, "but yes, eventually, we need it."

"I thought so."

"Taly?"

Taly looked down at little Sasha, who pulled on her sleeve.

"What is it, Sasha?"

"Is there creamed milk? Momma says it's rude to ask for more than we've already gotten, but you said to ask if we needed anything, so...."

He watched Taly smile down at the precocious little girl. Her color had improved since her treatment, as had her breathing.

"And you need creamed milk?"

Her dark curls bounced as she vigorously nodded her head. "I do. I really do."

"Well, then we'd better get you some." Taly looked back to Ranvir. "I'll see you later."

"You will," he told her.

She moved to help Sasha but felt his gaze on her long after.

∞ ∞ ∞ ∞ ∞

Ranvir entered the bridge to find Ganesha, Tane, and Pike exactly where they'd been hours ago. Fatigue added a slight droop to their shoulders, and their complexions were waning. A clear sign their energy levels were dropping dangerously low.

"I owe the three of you the greatest of apologies." Three heads turned toward him. "With everything that's happened and how fast it occurred, I never considered your conditions."

"You're questioning our capabilities?!" Pike's eyes narrowed from where he sat in front of the communications console.

"No," Ranvir immediately denied, "you all performed more than admirably, but we aren't familiar with one another because we are from different pods. Because of that, I don't know your energy consumption rate, which is unforgivable."

He moved to the panel Taly had mentioned beside the weapons console and opened it. Inside, exactly as she stated, was the power grip.

"Is that what I think it is?" Tane asked, turning his chair around for a better look.

"If you think it's a power grip, then yes. Talyani informed me several stations are spread across the ship, including two in the dining hall, which I used. You need to recharge, and then we'll plan our next steps."

Tane was the first to use the grip. Rising from the navigator's chair, he cautiously approached, but his need to refuel overrode his concern. He wrapped one hand firmly around the grip. As soon as it powered up, Tane jerked but didn't let go. A visible shiver rolled over his body. Less than a minute later, he released the grip looking at them in stunned amazement.

"That was amazing," he murmured, retaking his seat. "I'd recharge daily if I could use one of those."

"You should recharge no matter what source is available," Pike told him, stepping forward to take his place.

Ranvir noted it took Pike longer to reenergize, which meant his levels were lower than Tane's, or he had larger reserve capabilities and was storing for later.

Every cyborg who survived the transformation acquired a wide range of skills beyond those that came with being a cyborg. For some, it was size, others exceptional strength. A few could directly interface with computers. Ranvir had met others with those skills but never one with increased reserves.

Stepping back, Pike looked at Ranvir. "That felt amazing."

Putting the ship on autopilot, Ganesha crossed the bridge and grabbed the grip for his turn.

Ranvir couldn't get a read on the biggest cyborg among them.

Tane was obviously the youngest and most inexperienced of them. He probably hadn't been a cyborg for more than a year.

Pike was the hothead of the group. At least as much of a hothead as a cyborg could be, their cybernetics dampening their emotions.

Ganesha was the large silent type who seemed to observe and absorb everything around him. Ranvir could see him in a stealth pod, one that was inserted to gather the intelligence the rest of the pods in the Cyborg Elite Military Force needed. If it were true, it would make him a tremendous asset, but it could also make him a liability.

Before Shui's sham of a trial, there'd been rumors that the emperor had inserted cyborgs still loyal to him among them in the hopes of discovering more rebels.

Ranvir's cybernetic brain said that wasn't logical since Shui had decided to blow up their ships. His organic one said it was definitely something Shui would do. Shui would have sacrificed every cyborg to ensure no one survived to tell of his treachery.

Doubting another cyborg wasn't something Ranvir was used to doing, but he'd seen the cyborgs who stood beside Shui during the trial with his own enhanced eyes. Now was not the time to indiscriminately trust, especially with Taly on board. Her safety had somehow become his priority.

He waited for a reaction when Ganesha released the power grip and stepped back. The male stared at him for a moment, his gaze assessing. Finally, he said, "It will do."

"It'll do?" Tane looked at him in disbelief. "Are your nanobots defective?"

Ganesha spun around and took a threatening step toward the young navigator, causing him to lean back in his chair before Ganesha pulled himself up. "They are not," he said, returning to the pilot's seat but leaving the ship on autopilot.

Ranvir filed Ganesha's reaction away. There was something there, but he'd delve into it later. Right now, they needed to plan their next move. Walking to the captain's chair, he sat.

"Have you detected any ships?" He looked to Tane.

"No," Tane told him. "The only thing on the screen is the convoy, and they're moving away from us."

Good news.

"No one responded to the Celerity's distress call?" Ranvir's gaze went to Pike, sitting in Wells' spot, but Ganesha answered.

"No, and none of the convoy ships have broadcast that they lost a ship." At Ranvir's questioning look, Ganesha continued. "I've been monitoring the comms ever since we left Tyurma. I wasn't going to trust a non-cyborg. We all know Shui inserted spies among the prisoners. I wanted to make sure Wells wasn't giving away our location."

"And was he?" Ranvir asked.

Ganesha's expression darkened. "No, but I would have killed him if he had."

"That wouldn't have been your decision," Pike told him.

"Anyone that threatens a cyborg deserves to die," Ganesha spun in his chair to face the other cyborg.

"So you're judge, jury, and executioner now?" Pike challenged the larger cyborg. "Like Shui?"

"Of course not!" Ganesha denied. "But we've already been betrayed once. I won't be again."

"None of us want that." Ranvir's gaze traveled over the other three. "Which means we have to start trusting each other *and* Wells."

"I see you didn't include Mamsell Zulfiqar," Ganesha said, crossing his arms.

"Do any of you actually believe she'd betray us after everything she's done?" Ranvir gave him a disbelieving look.

"She did it to save another cyborg and *his* pod. She has no loyalty to *us*." Ganesha cocked his head to the side. "Is that why you are remaining close to her? To try and get her to switch her loyalties?"

It was apparent Ranvir's interactions with Taly hadn't gone unnoticed by the other cyborgs.

"No," Ranvir told him harshly.

"That's good to know." All four cyborgs turned to see Taly had somehow entered the bridge without any of them noticing. Something that shouldn't be possible. "Because that will never happen, but that doesn't mean I will betray any of you."

"You're the daughter of a Supreme Judge," Ganesha sneered.

"And I'm the sister of a cyborg," she fired back. At his shocked expression, she looked at Ranvir. "You didn't tell them?"

"It wasn't my place," he told her.

"Supreme Judge Zulfiqar doesn't have a son," Ganesha wasn't going to let this go.

"Nas isn't my father's son. He's my mother's from her first marriage to Major Reiji Demeter, Nas's father. My father had the records either altered or destroyed. I learned about Nas ten years ago. We've been in touch ever since."

"And Shui never found out?" Pike's eyes widened in disbelief.

"If he had, don't you think my parents would have been on one of the transport ships," Taly snapped back, her eyes angrily flashing at the weapons specialist.

"You don't think Shui would have put you on one?" Ganesha's question had her spinning around to face him.

"Oh, I'm sure he would have. Shui will destroy anyone who stands in his way in his quest for power."

"You know when it's discovered you're assisting the rebels, Shui will have your parents arrested if not outright killed," Ganesha continued to push.

Ranvir saw the anguish in Taly's eyes and wished there was something he could do to take it away but knew he couldn't.

"I know," she murmured, some of the fight going out of her. "I love my parents and wish I could change how this will affect them, but they knew what Shui was doing and chose to support him anyway. They'll have to suffer the consequences of that."

Silence reigned for several moments until Taly took a deep breath, straightened her shoulders, and looked at them. "So, is that enough to convince you I'm on your side?"

"It's enough," Ganesha said, "for now."

Ranvir wanted to deck the other cyborg, but Taly just rolled her eyes. "Whatever. So what's the plan? We obviously can't take all these people with us to Tuater."

All eyes went to Ranvir, who looked to Tane.

"What's the closest habitable planet to us?" Ranvir demanded.

Tane spun in his chair and pulled it up on the main screen. "Vemara is the closest."

"Vemara?" Taly's brows drew together. "Isn't that a desert planet?"

"Yes," Tane responded.

"But these people are colonists," she reminded them. "They were heading to Gamma-2, where the climate is perfect for agriculture. We can't leave them somewhere they have no chance of surviving."

"There's a spaceport there," Ganesha said dismissively. "If they still want to go to Gamma-2, they can arrange transportation."

"If they have the credits," she pointed out. "Most of these people spent everything they had getting passage on that ship. Now all they have are the clothes on their backs and whatever credits they were carrying when the pirates attacked."

"Vemara may have a spaceport, but it doesn't have what *we* need." Pike crossed the room and pulled up the weapon levels on that screen. All were below fifty percent. "We also need to replace the power crystals for the rear shields. Neither of those can be found on Vemara."

"Where can they be found?" Ranvir asked.

"Put the star chart on the main screen," Pike told Tane. When Tane did, Pike walked over and pointed to a small dot. "Yelmurn. It has a spaceport, but more importantly, we'll be able to acquire the power crystals and weapons without too many questions." He gave Ranvir a knowing look.

"And the colonists?" Taly asked.

"Will be able to find work if they cannot afford immediate passage," Pike told her.

"How long?" Ranvir demanded.

"Two days," Pike told him. "As long as we don't run into any more trouble."

Chapter Ten

Taly wasn't happy with the situation but knew it was the best they could do for the colonists. At least for now. Looking at Ranvir, she asked, "Ready to be shown your quarters?"

Ranvir had forgotten that was why she had come to the bridge in the first place. "The colonists are settled?"

"They are," she confirmed.

"Tane, anything on navigation?"

"No, Major."

"Then leave the ship on auto-pilot. Talyani's going to show us where we can rest." Extending his arm, he gestured for her to lead the way.

Taly led them to the door of the first suite and pressed a panel. "It's currently set so anyone can enter but can be changed if you want."

She waited until everyone had followed her in and gave them time to take in the two oversized couches, desk, chairs, and table before moving deeper into the suite.

"There is a food replicator next to the desk, but it contains mostly snack items and drinks. If you want a full meal, you'll want to use the ones in the dining hall. This door leads to the sleeping quarters." She led them into another room, smaller than the outer one but not by much. It contained a large bed and a small communications console. "There's a closet through that door," she pointed across the room, "and the bathroom is behind this one."

Taly stepped back to let them look into the bathroom. After they had, Ganesha finally spoke, "This will be more than adequate."

"Great." She clapped her hands together happily. "So, which one of you wants it?" She suddenly wanted to take a step back as four sets of intense eyes focused on her. "What?"

"Which *one* of us?" Ganesha asked carefully.

"Well, yes. Three other suites are available, along with the captain's quarters." She gave each one a disbelieving look. "You didn't think I expected all of you to sleep in the same room, did you?"

"This room alone is twice the size of what a pod normally shares," Ranvir told her.

"Seriously?" They didn't need to answer. She could see it in their eyes. "Well, it doesn't have to be that way now unless you want it to be. The other three suites are the same as this one, only done in different colors. The captain's quarters has a smaller bedroom and living area, but the bathroom is the same size."

"I prefer smaller rooms," Ganesha commented quietly.

"Okay, great, it's settled then. The rest of you can decide between this and the other suites."

It didn't take long after that for the rooms to be assigned. Pike took the one she'd shown them as it was the closest to the bridge. Tane chose the one across the corridor from it, which left the two closest to her suite.

"So which one do you want?" she asked, gesturing to doors on either side of the corridor.

Ranvir looked from them to the door behind her. "Where does that go?"

"That's my suite," she murmured, her voice suddenly husky as he took a step closer to her.

"Major."

Ranvir spun around, ready to protect Taly, before realizing it was only Tane coming out of his suite. "What is it?"

Tane's gaze traveled back and forth between Ranvir and Taly before answering. "I was wondering who you wanted on duty."

"You and Pike off for twelve," Ranvir told him.

"Yes, Major." He gave them a final look and reentered his suite, the door closing behind him.

"I assume that means you plan on taking the first twelve," she said quietly.

Ranvir turned back to face her. "Yes, Tane and Pike need rest."

"So do you." She reached up and placed a hand on his chest.

"I'll be fine for another twelve." He rested his hands on her hips, pulling her close.

"You're sure?" She didn't try to hide how concerned she was.

"I am." Reaching up, he cupped her cheek, his thumb gently moving over the shadows of fatigue beneath her eyes. "But you need to go rest."

"I do, and I will *after* I bring you and Ganesha something to eat. I know you've both recharged, but you still need something in your stomachs. Any requests?"

She could tell he would tell her not to bother, but apparently, he was learning that when she decided to do something, she did it. "I've always been partial to raten noodles."

"Northern or southern style?" she asked and smiled when his eyebrows shot up. "Several of my backup singers love them and always argue about which style is best, so the ship always has both."

"Southern."

∞ ∞ ∞ ∞ ∞

Taly quietly hummed the melody to one of her songs as she guided the hover cart down the corridor with four covered bowls of raten noodles. Two southern-style and two northern as Ganesha wouldn't tell her what he liked, insisting he wasn't hungry.

She'd found Vujcec in the dining hall, head down on a table, fast asleep. After waking him, she led him to one of the open suites. It was a testament to his exhaustion that he didn't even comment, just fell into bed fully clothed. It made her want to do the same, and she would as soon as she got this food to Ganesha and Ranvir.

"Here you go, guys," she announced as she entered the bridge. Ranvir immediately turned to her in the captain's chair while Ganesha remained facing forward.

"Four?" Ranvir asked, looking at the domed covers.

"I thought it should be more than enough for two hungry cyborgs."

He didn't know how to process her actions and went with the most straightforward response. "Thank you."

She grinned. "You're welcome. Oh, and I put Vujcec in the last suite on the right. He was asleep on his feet."

"I'd forgotten about him," which shouldn't happen with his cybernetic brain.

"He was a big help getting the colonists settled," she told him.

Ranvir nodded. "You need to get some rest, too."

"I'm heading for my suite now." She glanced at Ganesha. Seeing him occupied, she leaned down to whisper in Ranvir's ear. "Maybe you could join me after your shift is over."

It took a moment for Taly's words to register. When they did, his entire body stilled. Blood flowed to his cock as her lips brushed the top of his ear, her warm breath caressing his skin. There was only one answer. "I'd like that."

"Then it's a date," she told him before pulling back. Giving him one final teasing look, she left the bridge.

"For future reference," Ganesha told him, still facing forward. "You should let Mamsell Zulfiqar know all cyborgs have exceptional hearing."

"I will."

Ganesha finally turned in his chair and faced him. "Do you think it wise to become involved with her?"

Ranvir had never been good at expressing his feelings, even before becoming a cyborg. He especially wasn't good at doing it with someone outside his pod, but they needed to start building some trust if any of them were going to survive. If it took revealing his uncertainty, then so be it.

He took a deep breath and exhaled roughly. "No, but I'm drawn to her in a way I can't explain and isn't logical. Yet, I know I will willingly die to ensure she doesn't."

Ganesha studied him with an odd expression. "She's your cymar."

"My what?" Ranvir had never heard that term before.

"Cymar," Ganesha repeated. "It's the term the scientists who created us used for those of us who have the inexplicable need to protect someone when our processors say it's illogical. It means she's your mate. Not every cyborg has this defect."

"Mate," he murmured, both his brains swirling with confusion. It didn't feel like a defect. It felt like a necessity.

"Yes, the female who, if you'd met before becoming a cyborg, you'd have fallen in love with."

"You're saying I can't now?" Ranvir refused to believe that.

"I honestly don't know." Ranvir could tell the other cyborg was struggling to reveal what he knew. "I know of only one cyborg who had a mate and family before his transformation. He confided in me that it was difficult for him to feel the same depth of emotion as before."

"He was part of your pod." Now he understood Ganesha's conflict. He was revealing a confidence from a pod member.

"Yes. I saw her and their son in the assembly, but not him. I was able to keep them in my sights until boarding."

"They were on our transport?" Ranvir was surprised Ganesha was only mentioning this now.

"No." Ganesha's eyes flashed with an emotion Ranvir didn't understand. "They were loaded on the first ship. If they'd been on ours, I wouldn't have left that ship until I found them."

"I'm sorry, Ganesha." Ranvir found he indeed was.

"I can only hope Chas was on their ship." He stared at his hands fisted on his thighs.

"You never felt him reach out through your closed network at the trial?" Ranvir's brows drew together.

"No." Ganesha's head shot up. "Did you? With any of your pod members?"

"I did, but one by one, I lost them." Ranvir found that strange. "Is it possible there was a dampening system in place and on the ships making it so we couldn't use our closed network?"

He saw Ganesha seriously consider his question. "It's possible. We know Shui has been trying to hack our closed network. He could have discovered a way to impede the signal. It would force us to use the mainframe, giving him the chance to track us. Or the distance played a part."

"We need to find another way to reach out to those we trust."

"Agreed, but first, we need to reprogram our transponder and get our outgoing communications back up. We can't land on Yelmurn without them."

∞ ∞ ∞ ∞ ∞

Taly rolled onto her side and snuggled deeper into the warmth of her bed. The hard, firm warmth of her bed.

Wait.

Hard?

Firm?

Her bed wasn't either of those things.

Opening her eyes, the low light she'd left on revealed she was snuggled against a muscular chest, a naked muscular chest. Tipping her head up, her gaze met Ranvir's.

"You invited me to join you," he reminded her quietly.

"I did." Reaching up, she caressed his jaw. "Did I sleep twelve hours?"

"No. Pike and Tane only took eight and relieved us."

"That was nice of them." Her thumb brushed the CR branded into his flesh. "Does this hurt? Why haven't your nanobots healed it?"

"Not anymore." Capturing her hand, he brought it to his lips and kissed her palm. "The guards branding us let us know Shui specifically designed the ink so our nanobots couldn't heal it."

"Bastard."

"He wanted us marked as fugitives for the rest of our lives." Shui also knew it would make it easier for bounty hunters and assassins to identify cyborgs, but he wouldn't tell Taly that.

"Well, it doesn't. It shows you stood up against what you knew was wrong. That makes you a hero."

"We lost," he reminded her.

"Maybe the battle, but not the war." Rising on an elbow, she gave him a determined look. "Now, you can fight on your terms. Not Shui's."

"Those of us who survived are scattered across the universe, Taly, with no way of communicating without Shui being able to trace it."

Her mind started to race. "There has to be a way."

"There isn't.

Taly opened her mouth to continue to argue, then closed it. She could see the fatigue bracketing his eyes and realized this conversation could wait. Ranvir was exhausted.

"You need to sleep."

"I need something else more." Tilting his hips, he let her feel the rigid line of his cock.

"Damn, that's persuasive." She couldn't help rubbing against him, imagining how good it would feel to have *that* inside her instead of one of the toys she usually used. It had been a long time since she'd been with a man. "Unfortunately, right now, you need sleep more than sex."

Before he could argue, she laid her head on his chest, gently running a hand over it, and began to sing softly. She started with one of her favorite ballads, then moved on to another and another until she felt Ranvir's body relax, as much as a cyborg's body could, and he drifted off to sleep.

Rising slightly, she let her gaze travel over Ranvir, something she hadn't had the time to do. If she had, she would have realized how long his eyelashes were.

They were naturally longer than hers unless she was on stage wearing enhancers. They matched the darkness of the hair covering his head, long on the top, short on the side, although the ends were just a shade lighter. His eyebrows were dark slashes over eyes she knew were a golden brown.

His aristocratic nose and chiseled cheekbones made his lips appear softer and fuller. Taly couldn't help but wonder if he'd been born with those features or if his transformation had made them that way.

She'd noticed changes in Nas's features after becoming a cyborg. He'd broken his nose several times, so it had been crooked, but it was perfectly straight after his transformation. His cheekbones had also sharpened.

Her gaze traveled down the strong muscles of Ranvir's neck, across his broad shoulders to his smooth, heavily muscled chest that rose and fell as he slept. She was used to seeing half-dressed, well-toned males. The dancers in her show had to be in great shape to complete the complex moves her choreographer created, but they were slouches compared to Ranvir.

Muscle after muscle tapered down his body, disappearing beneath his briefs. Her fingers itched to follow those muscles down. She regretted insisting he sleep for a moment, but then he snored softly, and she knew he needed this. When was the last time he'd been able to sleep?

As carefully as possible, she moved across the bed. His big body took up a lot of space. Finally, she reached the edge and slid out without waking him. With one last lingering look, she headed for the bathroom.

Chapter Eleven

Ranvir went from asleep to alert in an instant. It was a skill he'd acquired long before becoming a cyborg. It had kept him alive when he lived in District Twelve. As a cyborg, his senses were even more enhanced, and they were feeding him vital information.

He was in Taly's suite. That came from his memory banks.

He was in Taly's bed. That came from his olfactory senses. Her distinctive scent surrounded him.

Taly wasn't with him. He felt the loss of her warmth in his soul.

How had that happened without him noticing? But more importantly, where was Taly?!

Surging out of bed, he began pulling on the clothing he'd left on the bench at the foot of the bed. His cybernetic processors calculated he'd slept seven point two five hours, more than enough for his organic brain to be refreshed. Pulling on his boots, he went in search of Taly.

He found her in the dining hall speaking to the colonists.

"I know Yelmurn isn't ideal," she was saying.

"Why can't you take us to Gamma-2?" a large, aggressive male demanded.

"Because that's not where *we're* going," Ranvir's gaze speared the vocal male as he crossed the room. The male retreated a step as Ranvir came to stand beside Taly. "It's thanks to Taly we're not leaving you on Vemara."

Shocked gazes filled the room, and he could tell they knew what that would have meant for them.

"We are grateful." Oved was the first one to speak. Ranvir recognized him as the male he hadn't left behind on the Celerity. "We're trying to understand our situation. Some of us have lost everything, so even if you did take us to Gamma-2, we wouldn't have the final payment needed to claim our land."

"But at least we could find work there," the male from the back argued.

"You can find work on Yelmurn, too," Taly assured him. "It also has a spaceport where you can book passage when you're able."

"But that could take *years*!" the same male exclaimed. "By the time we get to Gamma-2, our land will have been sold to someone else. There has to be more you can do for us!"

"More?" Ranvir's voice was so cold everyone took a step back. "You have your lives. Again, thanks to Taly. If that isn't enough for you, I'm more than willing to show you to an airlock."

"That... that won't be necessary," Oved stuttered, then looked to Taly. "Besides what some of us are saying," he glanced at the still muttering male behind him, "We are grateful for everything you've done, Taly."

With that, Oved urged the group out of the room. Ranvir waited until they were alone before rounding on Taly. "What were you thinking meeting with them alone?"

Taly frowned at that. "Why wouldn't I? They just wanted some information."

"Information that some of them weren't pleased to receive," he spat out.

"They just survived their ship blowing up," she reminded him. "They have the right to be upset."

"*You* survived a ship blowing up too, not once but twice. You're not whining and complaining," which shocked both halves of Ranvir's brains. He'd never encountered someone as selfless as Taly. It didn't compute with who her parents were, how she was raised, or the monumental fame she'd achieved.

She should be a selfish, spoiled debutante. But she wasn't, and despite what Ganesha had said, he knew he was falling in love with her.

"I...well, I guess I hadn't thought about it like that. I mean, I still have the Troubadour, and I..." she trailed off, giving him an uncertain look.

"And you?" he encouraged quietly.

Taly knew she was taking a risk, exposing herself like this. Which was funny, considering she'd been willing to risk her life to save Nas. Here she was risking her heart.

"Taly?" he prompted.

"I was going to say I have you. I just wasn't sure you'd want to hear that."

"Why wouldn't I?" he asked, wrapping his arms around her, pulling her close. "And you do. I crawled into your bed after all."

"Many males have tried to do that," she told him because it was true, but they weren't like Ranvir. They'd wanted to brag that they'd been with 'Talyani.' She'd learned that the hard way, which was why she hadn't been with a male in over three years.

"Are you saying I'm just another male in your bed?" he demanded, lifting her off her feet, so they were nose to nose.

"What?" Gripping his shoulders, she put a little distance between them. "No! Of course not."

"Then why did you say it?"

"Because it's been a long time since I've been in this situation." At his look, she shook her head at how ridiculous she sounded. "I don't mean *this* situation because obviously none of us have. I meant a male-female situation. A relationship."

"Why?" Ranvir found himself asking. "You're a beautiful, sexy, talented woman. Any male would be lucky to be with you."

"Not with me. They want to be with 'Talyani,' the image. That's what they want. All they see."

Loneliness filled her eyes, and Ranvir suddenly realized Taly's life was a lot like that of being a cyborg. People only saw what was on the outside and what the powers that be wanted them to see.

For Taly, they only saw a talented female they'd watched grow up. She was rich, beautiful, and lived a life of luxury they envied. For him, they saw a cold, emotionless, killing machine. One they needed but still looked at with fear and disdain. It made for a lonely life and relationships next to impossible. The two of *them* could have one if he were honest with her.

"I see you, Taly. *You.* Not *Talyani*, and it's you I want. Forever."

Taly searched his golden-brown eyes for the truth and found the vulnerability he was willing to reveal. She mattered to this male, could hurt him, and that was something she never wanted to do. "And I want you."

Leaning forward, she wrapped her arms around his neck as she captured his lips for a kiss that Ranvir quickly deepened. She wrapped her legs around his waist and rocked her hips against his growing erection. It's what she'd wanted to do before in her bed, but her concern for him had stopped her. Now nothing was stopping her.

Sinking one hand in her short curls, Ranvir changed the kiss angle while his other hand gripped her ass, grinding her against his cock. Gods, he was ready to explode, and he hadn't even gotten her naked.

"Oh, shit! Sorry!"

The exclamation turned their heads, ending their kiss but not their embrace. One of the male colonists quickly exited the dining room.

"I guess this isn't the best place to do this." With a regretful look, she unwrapped her legs from around him. For a moment, Ranvir didn't release her, then ever so slowly, he began to lower her, his cock pressing into her the whole way, causing her channel to clench with need. "Gods, Ranvir, I want you."

"Then let's go back to your suite."

"Major Somerled to the bridge. Major Somerled to the bridge." The call came through the ship's comm system.

Taly's forehead dropped against his chest. "The universe is plotting against us."

Closing his eyes, Ranvir fought to get his body back under control. His enhancements should have made it easy, but his body's physical desires overrode it for the first time. Taking a deep breath, his cock finally softened, and he relaxed his hold on her.

"It's not. It's what brought us together."

∞ ∞ ∞ ∞ ∞

"What did you need," Ranvir demanded, entering the bridge. Tane and Pike were where they'd been when he'd left the bridge to rest. The only new addition was Vujcec. He hadn't been able to talk Taly into coming with him.

Instead, she'd gone to medical, telling him there were some other children she wanted the med beds to treat. He didn't like leaving her alone, not how some of the colonists acted, but he couldn't convince her.

Before the door closed behind him, Ganesha rushed in. "What's wrong?"

"Nothing," Pike spun around in the captain's chair to face them. "I thought you'd like to know the outgoing communications array is back up and operational."

"You're saying we're identifiable!?" Ranvir asked deathly quiet.

"Yes." This time it was Vujcec who spoke. "As the Celerity."

Ranvir's brain worked on calculating how that was possible. "Explain."

"While you were on the Celerity, I hacked its systems and was able to download their data and codes, including their transponder code. We'll now appear as the Celerity on any navigation screen and in all communications."

"Good work, Wells." Ranvir missed the shock on the civilian's face at the praise as he turned to look at Tane. "Are there security protocols that will seal off sections of the ship?"

Tane went to the control console next to communications and drilled down through its menus. "Yes, by specific rooms and levels."

"Does it also give personal locations and numbers?"

"Yes." He turned back to Ranvir. "Why?"

"Several of the colonists aren't happy about being left on Yelmurn. They were aggressive with Taly, even going as far as to demand she should be doing more for them."

"More?" Vujcec's shock filled the room. "How much more do they think we can do? They know we're fugitives."

"Fugitives who can change their unfortunate circumstances if they turned us in," Ganesha told him.

"But we saved them." Vujcec couldn't believe anyone would do that.

"That was yesterday. Now they're worried about tomorrow." Ranvir looked back to Tane. "Taly's in medical. Can you isolate her signature so we can track her?"

"You actually think someone might harm her?" Vujcec asked.

"I'm not taking any chances." Ranvir watched Tane's fingers fly as he responded to Vujcec.

"There are currently five contacts in medical," Tane told him.

"She'll be near the med beds, near the control panel. She wanted to treat more colonists."

Triumph flashed over Tane's face. "Got her."

"I want an active trace on her at all times." Ranvir moved to take the captain's chair Pike had vacated. "When she leaves that deck, I want it sealed."

"Understood, Major."

"I'll go down and stay with her." Vujcec rose from his seat and headed for the door.

"You think you'd be any good in a fight?" Ganesha sneered as the civilian passed him.

Vujcec stopped and glared up at the cyborg. "Go ahead. Laugh. It's not like I haven't dealt with bullies like you my entire life. I know I'm short and skinny,

but I'm also scrappy, and while I may not win the fight, I can give Taly enough
time to get away."

A stunned silence filled the bridge as Vujcec stormed off. Ranvir found his
respect for the smaller male growing. No one knowingly or willingly took a
beating, but Vujcec was willing to for Taly. Ranvir just hoped it never came to
that.

"Get a trace started on Vujcec, too," he told Tane. "I don't want him left
down there when the deck is sealed."

"Done," Tane replied. "I've also logged all our signatures into the system."
It usually wasn't needed, as pods could always locate their members. It was
another reminder that they weren't one.

"We need to talk." Ranvir sat back in his chair, and the other three turned,
waiting for him to speak. "Ganesha and I discussed this last night during our
shift. Were either of you able to communicate with your pod members during
the trial?"

Pike and Tane looked at each other and replied, "No."

"And no one has felt the loss of a pod member?" Ranvir continued.

Again everyone responded no. "Then we need to assume they somehow
survived and will be looking for us, the same way we will be looking for them.
But for that to happen, *we* need to form a pod."

All three surged to their feet.

"No!"

"Fuck that!"

"Absolutely not."

Ranvir remained in his chair. He wasn't surprised by the outraged response
and raised his hands. "Hear me out."

"I'm not severing the link with my pod members," Pike growled. "They'll
think I died."

"I'm not asking you to," Ranvir told them. "What I'm proposing is that we
form a completely separate pod. It would mean we wouldn't have to rely on a
tracking program for locations. We would be able to communicate with one
another silently."

"That isn't possible," Ganesha told him. "All links must be severed before a
new pod can be formed."

"No, they don't," Ranvir countered. "It's highly recommended you do because you don't want an old pod member contacting you in the middle of an op, but it can't be forced."

"How do you know that?" Tane demanded.

"Because I was a member of Nas's pod, Talyani's half-brother, until I was promoted up and out to command my own pod."

"You never severed the link?" Pike gave him a disbelieving look.

"I did with everyone but Nas. We'd served together before becoming cyborgs, under Nas's father until he was killed."

"And it hasn't interfered with any of your ops?" Tane wanted to know.

"No. We only used it when we knew the other was on base."

"How did you accomplish this?" Ganesha asked, his brows drawing together.

"The same way we created the link with our original pod. By creating a firewall around a section in the communications area of our cybernetic brain, then granting our pod members access to it. There is no crossover between areas, so no personal or sensitive information is revealed."

"I need to think about this," Ganesha muttered.

"I expected nothing less, but consider this. Cyborg pods have always had a higher survival rate than lone cyborgs. It's why the military insisted we form them. We need to do this, or we may not survive long enough to find our lost pod members."

Chapter Twelve

Vujcec kept his eyes and ears open as he headed for medical. Last night, he'd been down here talking to the colonists, assisting them with the food replicators, helping them find quarters. He couldn't believe some of them acted as Somerled had claimed. Entering medical, he saw a baby in one of the med beds and Taly quietly talking to the couple reunited in the concert hall.

"She's going to be okay. I promise." Taly told the hugging couple.

"But I didn't even know she was sick," Sato sobbed. "We paid for a medic to check when she was six months old. He told us she was fine, just small."

"He placed her in a med bed?"

"Yes, but now that I've seen this one work, I don't think he turned it on. He placed Uki on the bed, secured her, and then went to the console." Sato gestured to the head of the bed. "After a moment, he told us all the readings were normal, and we had a healthy but small baby girl."

When the bed signaled it was done, Taly silently cursed the medic as she moved to the control console. He'd lied to this family. Her med bed had found many health issues in the tiny nine-month-old. Issues even a low-tech bed should have been able to detect and treat.

"Well, I can tell you from the readout I'm getting now that you really have a healthy little girl who will start growing normally." Pushing a button, the console printed out what it found, the treatments, and the prognosis. Walking back to Oved and Sato, who were now holding their daughter, she handed them the sheet. "Keep this for her records."

"Thank you, Taly." Sato pulled her close in a one-armed hug. "If there is anything we can ever do for you...."

"Don't worry about it. I'm just glad I could help. I wish you all a long and happy life."

Vujcec stepped to the side, nodding to the family as they left, before looking to Taly. "You just forever changed their lives."

"I shouldn't have had to if that medic had done his job," she spat out. "There's no way he scanned that baby."

"It happens a lot." At Taly's surprised look, he shrugged. "Med beds are expensive and wear out faster in the outer districts. Medics are ordered not to run them unless the patients are government members."

"Shui truly is a monster." If there was ever any doubt, it was gone.

"He is," Vujcec agreed, then gave her an uncertain look.

"What?"

"Can I ask you something?" he asked carefully.

"Sure." She moved to shut down the bed.

"Did a group of colonists complain we weren't doing more for them?" He found it hard to believe. He'd spent a great deal of time with them the night before. Well, some of them, mainly the families. Captain Ju and a few single males had quietly talked amongst themselves.

Sighing, she turned and looked at him. "Ranvir told you."

There was no need to lie to her. "Yes. So it's true?"

"Ranvir is a cyborg, Vujcec. They don't lie."

"They can," he reminded her. "How else do you think the rebellion was born?"

"By not answering," she sighed. "Which isn't the same as lying."

"I can't believe they'd feel that way." He came to stand beside her. "Do you know which colonists it was?"

"Feo. I recognized him from the concert hall. He was just as antagonistic there. He tried to stir the other colonists up and get them to believe we would sell them into slavery."

"What?!" His eyes widened. "What would make him think that?"

She shrugged her shoulders. "Who knows? He seems to be a guy who's used to intimidating and manipulating people."

"I know the type," he muttered.

"I think we all do," she agreed. "Hopefully, he'll calm down and stop trying to stir the others up."

"I doubt it, but at least we only have to put up with him for another day." He gave her a big grin. "I was able to reprogram the transponder code."

"You were?" She gave him a big smile. "Oh, Vujcec, that's great!"

"Yep, the Troubadour is now officially the Celerity."

That had her frowning. She'd seen what the Celerity looked like, and it wasn't anything like the Troubadour. "Will it stand up under scrutiny when we land?"

"On Yelmurn, yes," he reassured her. "It's not a very advanced planet. It only has a single level of security for identifying incoming ships. The transponder code. They don't visually inspect ships upon landing."

"Well, that's one less worry." She gave the brand on his face a serious look. "Have you tried to see if the med bed can remove that?"

"The guards said they couldn't be removed." He started to rise when her gentle touch stopped him.

"Ranvir said the same thing. That his nanobots couldn't heal it, but you're not a cyborg. Maybe the med bed can. It can't hurt to try."

Vujcec gave the bed a wary look.

"It's up to you," she said quietly.

Slowly, Vujcec moved to a bed and lay down after a moment's hesitation. Quickly going to the control console, Taly activated the bed and waited for the readout.

"What's it say?" Vujcec asked, wanting to squirm.

"It hasn't finished yet," she told him.

In a moment, it had. She held in a sigh of disappointment at the readings. While there was a list of things the bed could treat, the brand wasn't among them. Still, she pressed 'select all,' and the treatment began.

"Taly?"

"Let's just see what it does," she hedged.

Unfortunately, the "R" was still on his cheek when the bed finished. "I'm sorry, Vujcec."

"Don't be. I didn't expect it to work." He gave her a small smile as he sat up and slid his feet over the side of the bed, but she could tell it was forced.

"Still…"

"No, it is what it is." Getting off the bed, he gave her a quick hug and thought about Ranvir's concern for her being down here. "Want to go see what's happening on the bridge? We both know those cyborgs need all the help they can get."

Taly couldn't help but laugh. The first real laugh she'd had since this started. Sliding an arm around his waist, she turned toward the door. "You know, I think you're right. Let's go."

∞ ∞ ∞ ∞ ∞

Pike turned from his console to face the other cyborgs. "I've been able to locate a source for the power crystals we need for the shields and the weapons to be restocked. The dealer's willing to deliver both for an extra fee."

"Why are you saying it like that's a problem?" Ranvir asked.

"Because it is," Pike told him. "We can't get both."

"And why's that?" Ranvir queried.

"Because we don't have any credits," Pike explained. "So we'll have to decide which one's the priority. I vote for the weapons. They're harder to come by. But once we stiff the arms dealer, we'll have to take off immediately."

"Strip something off this pleasure cruiser and trade it," Ganesha said dismissively. "Problem solved."

"Excuse me?" a female voice said behind them.

Everyone turned to see Taly and Vujcec walking into the bridge. Ranvir glanced at Tane, who gave him a slight nod after securing the lower deck.

"No one is stripping anything off my ship unless they give me a damn good reason for it," Taly continued, not noticing Tane's actions.

"We need weapons and have no way to pay for them. Is that a good enough reason?" Ganesha told her.

"They don't accept credits?" She looked around the room in confusion. "I thought it was the universal currency."

"It is," Ranvir told her. "But, Taly, by now, Shui has frozen your accounts, and if he hasn't, then it's because he wants to track those credits to locate you."

"Then it's a good thing most of my funds aren't on Kirs."

"What?!" Five sets of eyes stared at her in shock.

Sighing, Taly shook her head. "Look, I know you guys think I'm some kind of pampered airhead who doesn't have a brain in her head. You think I just walk onto a stage, open my mouth, and sing.

"You don't understand the actual planning, logistics, and strategy involved. Yes, I have assistants, but someone has to tell them what to do, and that someone is me." She poked a finger into her chest. "I told you before I didn't go into this unprepared, and except for Shui trying to murder us, the plan has gone as planned."

"You need to explain this 'plan,' Taly." Moving closer, Ranvir ran a finger along her cheek. "We need to know."

She gazed up at him uncertainly. If Nas was here, she'd never reveal this, but he wasn't, and if any of them were going to survive, they would have to start trusting one another, starting with her. Sighing again, she moved and sat down in the captain's chair.

"Over the last few years, I got the impression that Nas wasn't happy being in the military. It's why I pushed for the MKX-10 when he suggested it. When he decided to leave, it would be the perfect ship for him."

"There's no leaving the military once you become a cyborg," Tane told her quietly, pulling her gaze to him.

She appreciated the sincerity she saw in his dark eyes. "I'm aware of that, but that doesn't mean someone couldn't slip away under certain conditions."

"They'd come after him," Ganesha said.

"I know that, too. We both did, so I used my 'deep-seated fear' of being abducted by pirates to convince the powers in the military to arm the Troubadour with military-grade weapons.

"After all, the loss of 'Talyani' would be a worldwide tragedy that would reflect badly on them and the emperor, and we all know what the emperor does to those who make him look bad."

Their disbelieving looks were starting to piss her off. "Seriously, do you really think I don't know how to work a crowd after all these years in the public eye? That I don't know how to find one person I need and play to their ego to get what I want? Arrogant generals are especially easy with their bloated egos. They like believing they're essential for protecting a defenseless little female from the big bad universe."

"You're talking about General Qubad," Ranvir didn't have to make it a question.

"*He's* the one who signed off on the arming of the Troubadour?" Pike gave them both a skeptical look. Qubad was the most-feared general in the Kirs Military.

"Yes, to both of you," she replied. "He was also the reason I was able to get two med beds."

"You're lying," Ganesha accused.

"Really?" Taly just raised an eyebrow at him as she stood, and before their eyes, her expression and body posture transformed into that of 'Talyani.'

"Oh, General, I need more than *one* med bed. The emperor wants me to sing at his annual ball, and I must travel back from Bionus to do it. What if I come down with one of those dreadful Bionus colds and the only med bed on my ship is broken? It takes *hours* for me to go through my vocal warm-ups. What if I'm late going on stage because I don't have *two* beds? You know how the emperor reacts when he's kept waiting."

Ranvir couldn't believe what he was seeing and hearing. The female before him was nothing like his Taly. Her breasts were upfront and prominent, her hip was cocked to one side, and her voice had taken on this sultry element that most would find sexy. To him, it was grating because he knew it wasn't the real Taly. His Taly.

"Shit..." Vujcec all but groaned. "Qubad never stood a chance."

Taly shrugged and her expression and body posture transformed back to the woman they'd gotten to know. "So that's how I got my two med beds and a fully stocked medical suite." She looked to Ganesha. "Believe me now?"

"I believe you're a good actress, and while *entertaining*," Ganesha sneered that last word, "it doesn't explain the credits you claim to have."

"You don't have to have a cybernetic brain to know that eventually, Nas needed to refuel and restock the Troubadour. So I ensured he'd have all the credits he'd need."

"How?" Ranvir asked, bringing her attention back to him.

"I began rerouting funds to different places then downloading them onto untraceable credit strips."

"And no one noticed?" Vujcec asked. Everyone knew how closely Shui monitored the financial systems of Kirs.

"They were always in small amounts to not draw attention and through fictional touring expenses. The news streams always report how lavish and extravagant my lifestyle is." She saw understanding cross Vujcec's face. "So those expenditures were never questioned."

"You're saying you can access enough credits right now to pay for the weapons and power crystals we need for the shields, *and* we could acquire additional fuel rods if we want?" Ranvir asked carefully.

"Yes." A sick feeling began to grow in her stomach at their disbelieving looks. Had she miscalculated? "How many credits are you talking about?"

"Between the weapons and crystals," Pike quickly calculated, "five million credits. If we pick up extra fuel rods, add another million."

"Really?!" she asked, relief rushing through her.

"Taly..." Ranvir began to tell her supplies in space were expensive, especially weapons.

"I thought it would be an unreasonable amount," she talked over Ranvir.

"Five million credits is reasonable to you?" Vujcec squeaked.

"Well, it might be a little high, but I figured there'd be some mark up this far from Kirs." The silence in the room started to get to her, so she demanded, "What now?"

"Taly." Ranvir carefully gripped her shoulders, turning her, so she faced him. "Are you telling me you have five million credits on board the Troubadour?"

"No." She immediately replied and saw his shoulders sag. "I'm telling you that amount won't even put a dent in what I have on the Troubadour."

"That's not possible."

Ranvir tried to step in front of Taly as Ganesha moved toward her, but Taly had already stepped around him and crossed the room. She didn't stop until she stood toe-to-toe with the deadly cyborg.

"Do you know how many credits I made for winning Worlds?" she demanded angrily but didn't let him answer. "Ten million, and that was ten years ago. Do you know how many I clear as pure profit from just one of my concerts? Between 1 to 5 million, depending on the size of the crowd. Do you know how many of those concerts I put on a year? Seventy-five to one hundred. Now multiple that by the ten years I've been touring. I'm sure even your cybernetic brain can calculate how much that would be, and that's without any royalties from my albums."

Vujcec moved to a chair and sank into it. "Gods, Taly. I knew you pulled in the credits but not at that level. I can't believe the news feeds and social media platforms never got a hold of that."

She turned away from Ganesha, who'd lost his aggressive attitude, to Vujcec. "They couldn't because Nas showed me how to hide the funds in multiple accounts. The official one for 'Talyani' only received ten percent of my earnings after the first few years."

"Nas has been watching over you for a long time." Ranvir wasn't sure how he felt about that, especially since Nas had never once mentioned it to him, and he considered the other male the closest thing to family he'd ever had.

"He has," she agreed, then looked to Pike. "So, how do you need the credits? On a credit strip that can be verified or as a direct transfer?"

"A credit strip for each. That way, it's not traceable back to us."

"Just let me know the amounts, and I'll get them to you. So it's agreed," her gaze traveled around the bridge, "nothing is getting stripped off my ship."

"Agreed," everyone said at once.

"Good. Is there anything else I need to know about?" When everyone responded in the negative, she nodded. "Then I'm going to my suite."

Chapter Thirteen

"Damn, I think I'm in love."

Tane's low murmur had Ranvir seeing red. Grabbing the younger cyborg by his neck, Ranvir pulled him out of his chair and threw him across the room. Tane hit the security room door, denting it before he slid to the floor, a stunned look on his face. As Ranvir advanced, meaning to beat the crap out of the little shit, Ganesha and Pike grabbed his arms and pulled him away.

"She's mine!" Ranvir roared, struggling against the hands holding him.

"What?!" Tane gave him a confused look. He replayed what he'd said in his mind and paled. "I wasn't serious, Major! Taly's great, but she's not for me."

"No, she's not!" Ranvir continued to struggle. "She's mine!"

"Anything you say, Major." Tane raised his hands in surrender.

"You need to go cool off, Major." Ganesha and Tane muscled him to the doors of the bridge and shoved him through it. Before it closed, Ganesha told him. "Go see your cymar and get it out of your system."

"What's a cymar?" Tane asked, rising from the floor.

∞ ∞ ∞ ∞ ∞

Ranvir's cybernetic brain flashed multiple warnings that he wasn't acting rationally, but he overrode them because his human brain kept replaying Tane's words on a continuous loop. Taly was his and only his, and he would make sure everyone knew it, especially Taly. Moving down the corridor with cybernetic speed, he burst into her suite.

Taly strode from her bedroom wearing a loose flowing yukata that revealed a great deal of leg and cleavage. "Ranvir, is something wrong?"

He didn't answer, storming across the room. Her eyes widened before he swept her into his arms and carried her back the way she'd come.

"Ranvir!"

"You're mine!" he growled, tossing her onto the bed. He followed her down, her soft, lush body conforming to his harder one. Sinking a hand in her silky curls, he leaned down and claimed her lips in a hard, hungry kiss.

Taly wasn't sure what had happened between her leaving the bridge and Ranvir arriving in her suite, but whatever it was, she wasn't going to complain. She'd been thinking about this ever since their first kiss.

Ranvir knew Taly deserved better than this. She deserved to be treated like the treasure she was, but he was losing control. Ripping his mouth away from hers, he tried to regain it only to have it shredded further when she whispered, "More, Ranvir. I want more."

He gripped the top of her yukata with one hand and ripped it open, exposing her naked beauty to his hungry gaze for the first time. Gods, she was gorgeous.

"Now you," she demanded, pulling at the hem of his shirt.

In an instant, he was up, his clothes disappearing. Then he was back, wedging his hips between her thighs. The position opened her entirely to him and let his hard throbbing cock settle over her clit. Bracing himself on his elbows, he flexed his hips against hers, coating his cock with her slickness again and again.

"Gods, Ranvir, that feels so good! Don't stop!" She rocked her hips against him, creating even more friction on her clit.

Her breathless words ended his control. Pulling back, he notched the head of his cock at her opening and thrust, filling her with one hard stroke.

"Shit!" Her tiny gasp did what all his cybernetic enhancements could not. It froze him in place.

"Taly?" He searched her face taking in her tightly closed eyes and pinched mouth. Gods, how could he have done that to her? She was so much smaller and more delicate than him. For him to forget was unforgivable.

"Just... just give me a minute," she panted.

Ranvir would give her anything she asked. Slowly, she relaxed, and her crystal blue eyes opened, staring into his. He saw the same need, desire, and passion he felt for her in them. Still, he remained absolutely still.

Until she wrapped her legs around his waist and pulled him even deeper, incinerating his immobility. Keeping his eyes locked with hers, watching for any sign of discomfort, he began to thrust into her hot, slick depths with a forceful rhythm.

Her groan of pleasure told him everything he needed to know. "More. Harder."

Her encouragement was all it took for him to release the last shred of control he held. Interlacing his fingers through hers, he stretched her arms over her head, withdrew almost entirely, and surged back into her hot depths, giving her what she demanded, what he'd wanted since he'd first met her.

"Oh, Gods!" She couldn't stop her legs from tightening around him, her hips from gyrating, trying to keep him right *there*. It had been so long since she'd done this, and it hadn't been anywhere near this amazing. She knew she wouldn't last long, not how Ranvir was hitting her clit.

Ranvir felt his balls tightening and knew he was close, but he refused to go without her. Leaning down, he captured one of her breasts, sucking it deep into his mouth as he changed the angle of his thrusts. The dual assault had her entire body tensing beneath him, her legs pulling him impossibly deeper. She screamed his name seconds later. Her channel clamped painfully down around him. It had his orgasm roaring through him, and with one final thrust, he exploded.

∞ ∞ ∞ ∞ ∞

Taly lay draped over Ranvir's chest, breathing hard and listening to his pounding heart slowly resume its normal pace. Before he collapsed, he'd rolled onto his back, pulling her on top of him.

Absently, she ran her hand over his chest and tried to pull her scattered thoughts together. She'd never experienced an orgasm like that before. It had been more than physical. She swore she'd felt Ranvir touch her soul. Whoever had said cyborgs were cold and emotionless had obviously never been with one. Ranvir was the most passionate male she'd ever met. It might be hidden beneath a cool exterior, but it was there.

Feeling Ranvir's arms tighten, she lifted her head and found concern-filled brown eyes staring at her. Reaching up, she cupped his cheek. "I'm fine, Ranvir."

"I didn't harm you?"

"Of course not," she immediately denied. "Why would you think you did?"

"I lost control."

"Which I thoroughly enjoyed." The small smile she gave him turned serious as she asked. "Are you okay?"

"Me? Of course, I am."

"You were upset when you arrived." She reminded him. "Why? What happened?"

"Just a misunderstanding with Tane," he told her. "It has been resolved."

Pushing up so her elbows rested on his chest, her gaze searched his. "A misunderstanding that had you storming into my suite? Throwing me on my bed? And claiming I'm 'yours'?"

"Are you not?" he demanded.

"I'd like to be," she murmured, gazing uncertainly at him. "But..."

"But what?"

"But if we are going to do this, be together, then we have to be honest with each other. And right now, you're lying to me."

"I'm not *lying*. A lie is a false statement told to deceive deliberately. I did not do that."

"No, you didn't. You also aren't telling me what the disagreement was about." Seeing the stubborn set of his jaw, Taly pushed away from him and moved to get out of bed.

She didn't know why she was pushing this. Probably because she needed something, just one thing she could be sure of when the rest of the universe was against them. She'd thought Ranvir could be that. Now she wasn't so sure.

Sitting up, Ranvir turned her around to face him. "It means that much to you? To know?"

"Yes. People have lied to me my whole life, Ranvir. My parents. My agents. It was always with good reasons, but those reasons have always benefited *them*, not me, and now for the first time in my life, I can truly do what I want."

"And what you want is to be told the truth." His gaze searched hers wanting to be sure.

"Yes." She told him, not a hint of doubt in her voice.

"Tane claimed he thought he was in love with you," he finally told her.

"What?!" She'd never given the cyborg the slightest bit of encouragement.

"It enraged me, thinking he was trying to lay claim to you. I would have killed him if Ganesha and Pike hadn't stopped me."

Taly could understand his reaction because if the situation were reversed and another female said that about Ranvir, she'd want to claw her eyes out. Ranvir was hers.

Rising on her knees, she framed his face with her hands. "I'm not interested in anyone but you, Ranvir." She leaned in and lightly kissed his lips. "Just you." She kissed him again. "Only you."

Straddling his thighs, she pushed him onto his back as her hands explored his body. His pecs flexed as her nails lightly grazed his skin, leaving faint marks. Leaning down, she gently kissed the minor injuries before dragging her tongue over one of his dark, flat nipples, nipping at it until it hardened, then moved on to the other.

"Taly..." he groaned, all his circuits overloaded again. Rising to rest on his elbows, he asked, "What are you doing?"

"I'm exploring what's mine." She lifted uncertain eyes to his. "You are mine, aren't you?"

"Yes," he immediately assured her. He never wanted her to doubt that for even a second.

That was all she needed to continue kissing her way down his incredible body. She knew Ranvir's physiology had changed when he became a cyborg. The transformation made them stronger and more muscular, but she doubted few had as well-defined abs as Ranvir.

Sliding down Ranvir's legs, her mouth traversed the hard peaks and deep valleys of those abs arrowing down his body, giving each one the attention it deserved until his cock nudged the bottom of her chin. Dropping her head, she rubbed her cheek along Ranvir's hot, satiny cock, taking in his dark, spicy scent that comforted her as much as it aroused her.

Easing back slightly, she saw a glistening bead of precum just starting to leak from the tip of his stiff cock. Swooping down, she captured it with her tongue before it began to drip down his slit. He tasted as spicy as his scent. It had her channel clenching with need and her taste buds wanting more. She swirled her tongue around the head of his cock, making sure she didn't miss a drop, then opened her mouth as wide as she could and took him in.

"Taly!" Ranvir's hips bucked up before he could prevent them. Sending his cock deep into her hot, moist mouth. Yet when he tried to pull back, Taly gripped the base of his cock, holding him still as she took him even deeper.

With each stroke, her tongue caressed the thick pulsing vein underneath his cock, building both their desires.

"Gods, Taly!" Ranvir sank his fingers into her hair and watched her mouth take his cock. He'd never seen anything as erotic as Taly's lips stretched around his cock, her cheeks hollowing out as she sucked him.

"Don't stop!" he gasped, his breathing becoming ragged as his hips pumped faster and faster into the hot depths of her mouth. He could feel his balls tightening, and when she took him deep into her throat and swallowed, he exploded, sending his seed streaming down her throat.

Taly eagerly swallowed every drop Ranvir gave her, savoring the taste, knowing she would be coming back for it often. Slowly, she eased back, his now flaccid cock slipping from her mouth. Looking up, she couldn't help but smile. Ranvir's eyes were closed, his mouth hung open, and his chest heaved. She had totally destroyed the most powerful cyborg she'd ever met. How many women could say that?

Ranvir fought to regain control of his breathing and other systems after the most explosive orgasm he'd ever experienced. He hadn't expected *this* when he'd come to Taly. He'd been enraged. She should have been terrified of him, screamed for help, and attempted to fight him off.

But she'd done none of those things. Instead, she'd accepted him, not only into her body but into her life, allowing him to claim her. She was his cymar, even if she didn't know it. Yet.

Feeling Taly move, he opened his eyes to find her smiling at him. He couldn't help but smile in return.

"Feeling pretty proud of yourself, are you?" he asked.

"I am," she told him sassily, then let out a little shriek when he picked her up and rolled her onto her back. "Ranvir!"

"You're my cymar, Taly."

Taly stilled, her eyes searching his golden-brown ones. "You're what?"

"Cymar," he repeated. "It's the cyborg term for mate. It means I know I will love you forever, will protect you, and willingly die for you."

"Oh, Ranvir." She made no effort to hide the tears that filled her eyes as she stretched up to brush her lips against his. "I love you, too, and know I will forever."

Chapter Fourteen

Taly couldn't keep the smile off her face as she headed for the lower deck. Ranvir had tried not to wake her when he'd gotten out of bed to relieve Ganesha on the bridge.

He'd encouraged her to sleep longer, but she couldn't. It seemed she was already addicted to him holding her while she slept. After he left, she rose, showered, and dressed. Then she headed out to check on the colonists. They would be arriving on Yelmurn soon, and she wanted to do what she could for them.

The Troubadour was fully stocked for her and the support personnel who always traveled with her. It included food, hygiene supplies, and bedding. Things the colonists would need to start a new life. She and the guys could survive with what was stored on the upper deck.

She came to an abrupt halt, nearly running into the door to the stairwell that led to the lower deck when it didn't open. It was supposed to do that automatically. Why hadn't it?

Reaching to the side, she pressed the secondary release button, and the door remained closed. Frowning, she turned and headed for the bridge.

"Ranvir, do you know why..." she trailed off as she entered the bridge and took in the solemn faces and the tension in the room. "What's happened?"

It took a moment for anyone to respond. Finally, Ranvir turned in the captain's chair to look at her. "Reports are coming in that a group of cyborgs has been captured."

"Who?" she whispered, a sick feeling growing in her stomach.

"We don't know," he said.

"Shui has ordered their execution be broadcast live," Pike told her in an emotionless voice.

Seeing Taly pale, Ranvir immediately stood and went to her side, pulling her into his arms. He glared at Pike over her head as she burrowed into his chest. "We don't know who they have," he tried to reassure her. "Or even if it's true."

"When?" she asked, pulling back slightly to look up at Ranvir.

"Within the hour," he told her.

"Do we know how they were captured?" she asked, looking to Pike.

"Bounty hunters," Ganesha answered from the pilot's seat, turned to face the rest of the room, having set the ship on autopilot.

"But *how*?" she demanded. "They're cyborgs, for Gods sake. They should have been able to handle a few bounty hunters."

"That's unknown." Ranvir ran a comforting hand up and down her back. "And there's no way to find out. Not without giving away our location."

She frowned up at him. "What do you mean? Vujcec told me he changed our transponder code."

"He did, but we'll draw undue attention if we start asking too many questions," Ranvir told her. "We can't have that. Especially when we're arriving on Yelmurn in less than a day."

"But if there was a way?" Taly asked. "To communicate with other cyborgs. One that couldn't be traced."

"That's not possible," Vujcec said from where he sat. "It would have to be routed through multiple comm satellites on previously established and encrypted channels. Only members of the Kirs High Command can do that, and even if you had all that, there still has to be someone on the other end who knows how to open it."

"All true," she readily agreed, "but if such a channel existed...."

It was Ranvir's turn to frown. "Taly. Are you saying you have access to an encrypted channel?"

It wouldn't surprise him if she did, not after everything else she'd been able to accomplish.

Sneaking onto a prison ship.

Freeing them.

Getting her hands on the most advanced ship ever produced and having it fully loaded with weapons.

Access to an encrypted channel was nothing compared to any of those things.

"Yes," she told him. "Nas set it up so we could communicate freely, but it's not a live channel. He said those were continually monitored."

"Then how..." Ranvir began.

"Of course!" Vujcec cut Ranvir off. His eyes gleamed with excitement. "Why didn't I ever think about that before?"

"What are you talking about?" Tane demanded.

Ganesha spoke quietly before Vujcec could. "Messages. Nonvisual ones only take a nanosecond to transmit, making them impossible to track on encrypted channels."

"How do you know that?" Ranvir gave him a suspicious look.

Ganesha and Ranvir locked eyes for several tense moments before Ganesha finally answered. "It was how I used to receive my orders from high command."

"You and your pod were one of the emperor's assassin squads." It suddenly all made sense to Ranvir. The secretive vibe he got off Ganesha. The way the other cyborg struggled when he spoke of his pod members. Spinning around, he shoved Taly behind him, whipped out his blaster, and aimed it at Ganesha.

"Shui's assassin squads are a myth." Ganesha's tone remained casual even as he stood, his gaze traveling over the room. "Assassins are never part of a pod. It's why Shui believed they'd always remain loyal to him."

"And are you still?" Ranvir demanded. "Loyal to him?"

"I'm here, aren't I? Branded just like you?" Ganesha gestured to the CR on his cheek.

"You didn't answer the question." Ranvir's finger tightened on the trigger.

Taly stepped away from Ranvir, giving him room to move if needed because she'd heard about Shui's assassins. Nas had warned her about them. He'd said they should never be trusted. It was rumored that medics tampered with parts of their organic brain to remove their sense of right and wrong during their transformation. That way, they'd follow whatever order they were given, no matter how heinous.

Ganesha hadn't seemed cold-blooded and without decency to her. Sure, she hadn't known him long, and they didn't like each other, but he hadn't done anything against them either. He'd even supported her when she'd insisted they needed to defend the Celerity against the pirate attack. Why would he do that if his mission was to turn them into the emperor?

"Ganesha?" She moved around Ranvir to make eye contact with the other cyborg.

"Taly, stay behind me," Ranvir ordered, catching her movement from the corner of his eye.

Ganesha also followed her, his dark eyes zeroing in on her position.

"What is your question, Mamsell Zulfiqar?" Ganesha asked formally.

"Why are you here?" she asked.

"Because I was in the same cell you rescued us from," he told her, the corners of his mouth curving up ever so slightly.

"That's not what I meant, and you know it," she pointedly.

"I honestly doubt anyone knows what's going on in your mind, Mamsell Zulfiqar. If you want to know something specific, ask a specific question."

"And you'll answer truthfully?" she asked, crossing her arms over her chest.

"Yes."

"You can't trust the word of one of Shui's assassins," Pike spat, pulling his own blaster.

"Is that what you are, Ganesha? One of Shui's assassins?" Taly asked.

Ganesha's gaze, which had shot to Pike, returned to her. Everyone on the bridge waited for his answer.

"I was," he finally admitted quietly, making no excuses. "Now, I am not."

"How can we possibly believe that?!" Pike demanded. "It's known that Shui placed spies amongst those he accused of treason."

"Think!" Ganesha ground out, his gaze traveling around the bridge. "Those rumors might have been true if Shui had planned on letting us reach Tyurma. But his ultimate plan was to murder us and blame it on the rebels. Why would he risk loyal resources in a situation like that? Especially when he knew there were still unidentified rebels out there."

"What caused him to consider you a rebel then?" Taly asked.

He looked back at her but didn't maintain eye contact. "I refused to take out a target."

"What target?" Ranvir demanded, his blaster still aimed at Ganesha.

Ganesha's gaze bore into Ranvir's as he responded. "One who Shui was certain would cause the entire populace of Kirs to rise up in outrage against the rebels when it became known they were responsible."

"There's no one with that much influence," Tane immediately denied, but Ranvir's eyes widened when Ganesha's gaze returned to Taly.

"There is," Ganesha refuted, "and if you'd listened to all the transmissions we've received, you'd realize Shui is already spreading rumors that she's been abducted."

"She?" Tane frowned at that.

"Oh, my Gods!" Vujcec's eyes widened, and he jumped to his feet and looked at Taly. "It's *you*!"

"What?" Taly's gaze flew from Vujcec to Ganesha in confused disbelief. "Me? Why?"

"For the reason, I just stated," Ganesha told her. "Not only are you the daughter of a Supreme Judge who supports Shui, many consider you a member of their own family, having watched you grow up. You are considered Kirs' greatest treasure, with supporters who outnumber Shui's. Your death, at rebel hands, would shift support to the emperor."

A stunned silence filled the bridge after Ganesha finished.

∞ ∞ ∞ ∞ ∞

Taly just stared at Ganesha in disbelief. He hadn't just said what she thought he'd said.

Had he?

Shui couldn't have been targeting her for assassination.

It made no sense. Sure, she knew she was popular. Yes, many considered her 'family' because of the Worlds competition. Still, to have her murdered. Just to advance his own position and sick agenda?

"When?" she whispered, wondering how long she'd lived on borrowed time.

"Last month while on Bionus," he told her bluntly.

"The tour I postponed after overhearing my parents discussing what Shui was planning," she whispered.

"Yes. Shui felt it would change the minds of those reluctant to invade Bionus."

"Bastard." Taly could totally see Shui doing that. She lifted her chin, challenging him, "So you didn't refuse to murder me. You just never had the opportunity. Are you going to complete your mission now?"

The corners of Ganesha's mouth curved up slightly. He'd never understood why others found her so fascinating, even after watching her vids. Yes, her songs were always filled with emotion and conveyed the hopes and dreams of many in their world. Cyborgs weren't supposed to have feelings. They especially weren't supposed to be ruled by them. It's why the Cyborg Elite was created in the first place. So problems didn't arise as they did in the 'regular' military.

He'd been shocked when he realized *she* was the one saving *him*. Unintentional, though it might be. She'd saved him, and he never forgot a debt. He was breaking every code painfully drilled into him to answer her truthfully.

"No. I failed in my mission when I refused to kill you two weeks ago while you were at the hospital."

"What?!" Taly's mind whirled, and her eyes widened when she realized when that was. "I was visiting the *Children's Hospital*!"

Ganesha nodded. "Yes. My orders were to blow up the building while you were inside."

"You obviously refused," Ranvir said, lowering his blaster so he could pull a shocked Taly into his arms. If it hadn't been for this cyborg, this assassin, he never would have found his cymar.

"No," Ganesha gave him an unfathomable look. "If I had, Shui would have sent someone else. I simply failed to complete my mission."

"Which is why you were branded a rebel," Vujcec whispered, and Ganesha nodded, acknowledging his reasoning.

"Why didn't you?" Taly asked from the safety of Ranvir's arms. "Kill me, that is. I'm nobody to you."

"Correct," he agreed, "but you aren't to those children. Even a cyborg trained to be an assassin knows children are the ones we were created to protect."

"And if I had performed on Bionus?" She couldn't stop herself from asking.

Ganesha shrugged his shoulders. "Then the outcome would have perhaps been different."

Taly wasn't sure how to respond to that. On the one hand, she trusted Ganesha. After all, he was now a rebel, too. On the other, he'd just admitted to being one of Shui's assassins. Could you ever completely trust someone like that? She stepped out of Ranvir's arms.

"Are you planning on murdering me now?" He had said to ask specific questions. That he'd answer honestly. She wasn't sure she'd like what he'd say.

Ganesha was across the room before anyone could react. Shocking everyone when he dropped to his knees before her. "I, Thanos Ganesha, pledge my life and loyalty to you, Talyani Zulfiqar. There is no command you give that I will refuse until the day I meet the Gods. And if they refuse me because of what I've done, I will be yours for all eternity."

Taly's shocked gaze went from Ganesha at her feet to Ranvir, who had moved to her side. She knew those words. It was a pledge from a select segment of the population on Kirs. They followed a specific belief system that supported the idea that ancient warriors had made vows to the Gods when they fought together against the great evil that tried to take over the universe.

Saying such words for them was never taken lightly because the cost to one's eternal soul was too great. For Ganesha to say such a thing to her...

No one on the bridge could doubt his sincerity.

Chapter Fifteen

"It shouldn't be sent directly from the Troubadour," Vujcec argued. "There's a chance they could find the Celerity's transponder code."

"It will be on an open channel. Wouldn't it draw *more* attention if there wasn't a code?" she argued.

"But it shouldn't be the Celerity's," Vujcec continued to argue.

Things were still tense between the cyborgs on the bridge, and Taly knew that wouldn't end anytime soon, but she trusted Ganesha's words. She had to. She refused to become like Shui, who murdered anyone who gave him a moment of doubt.

"What are you talking about, Taly?" Ranvir remained close to his cymar while keeping an eye on Ganesha. "You said you and Nas had access to an encrypted channel."

"We do, and we'll be using it, eventually, but to let Nas know I need to contact him, I first need to send out a message on a specific channel he continually monitors."

"What kind of message?" Ganesha asked.

Ranvir tensed when she turned to look at him.

"Just something ordinary like, 'Hi, Big Brother, things are good here. How's it going for you?'"

"That's it?" Vujcec questioned, giving her a shocked look.

"Yes. I send it, then I wait."

"Has he ever not responded?" Ranvir asked.

Taly shook her head. "No, but once, it took several days because he was on a mission."

"So when he responds, how does he know where to send the message?" Vujcec asked.

"We have a prearranged account it goes into, also encrypted. I enter the code for a safe channel I can be reached at, as does he. Then it's forwarded to both of us, and voila, we're in direct contact."

She took in the disbelief on everyone's faces, including Vujcec's, and sighed, "What?"

"Not even I used that intricate of a way to communicate when on a mission," Ganesha said quietly.

"How long have you and Nas been communicating like this?" Ranvir asked, pulling Taly's attention away from Ganesha.

"Since I was sixteen," she told him absently, giving Ganesha a considering look before turning back to Ranvir. "It was usually only once or twice a year until I told him I was considering getting a private transport. After that, he began contacting me monthly, making suggestions and giving me advice."

"He must have suspected something like this would happen and wanted to make sure you were protected," Ranvir murmured, silently thanking Nas as he pulled her in close, gently kissing the top of her head.

If Nas hadn't, he wouldn't be holding this incredible female in his arms. Hopefully, he'd get the chance to do it in person.

"Which is why I have to get this message out." Taly tipped her head up, her eyes pleading with his. "I have to make sure he's okay, Ranvir."

"And you will, but Vujcec's right. It shouldn't be sent directly from the Troubadour, even with a different transponder code." He placed a finger across her lips, stopping the argument he knew was coming. "I'll send it from a public terminal once we're on Yelmurn. That way, there's no chance it can be traced back to us."

Taly pulled back to frown at him. "What do you mean *you'll* send it?"

"You don't think I'm letting you get off this ship on Yelmurn, do you?" He gave her a disbelieving look. "You might be recognized."

"*I* might be recognized?!" Taly pulled out of his arms to glare at him. "Me? I'm not the one with the brand on my cheek! As for *letting* me off *my* ship, I'll come and go as I please! Thank you very much."

Ranvir knew he wasn't acting logical, but where Taly was concerned, he couldn't be. She was his entire world now and if keeping her safe meant she was pissed at him, so be it.

"Be that as it may, you will remain on the ship. It's too dangerous for you on Yelmurn."

"Why? Because I have a bounty on my head? Oh, wait," she threw her arms up in an exaggerated motion before jabbing a finger in his chest, "that's *you*."

"We are trained to handle such danger," he reminded her. "You're not."

"So were those cyborgs Shui's going to execute any minute now!" Her voice broke, and she had to turn away as tears filled her eyes. Damn it. She wasn't going to cry right now. Tears solved nothing. But just the chance of Nas being one of those cyborgs...

Ranvir hated seeing her upset like this and realized this was why she was being so stubborn. She was scared her brother was about to die. Engulfing her in his arms, he tried to reassure her. "Nas is too smart to be caught by bounty hunters, Taly. You know that."

Taly silently nodded against his chest.

"Umm, guys," Vujcec interjected, reminding them they weren't alone.

Looking over his shoulder, Ranvir demanded. "What?"

"The broadcast is beginning. Do you want me to...?"

"Put it on the main screen," Taly told him. She made no move to wipe away her tears as she turned in Ranvir's arms and faced forward. She was going to need his support if Nas appeared on the screen.

The main screen flickered before it cleared, revealing grey metal walls and a transparent one. It had all four cyborgs viciously cursing.

"What?" she asked.

"That's a maintenance room on the Nissa," Ranvir told her in a tight voice. "Technicians use it to make external repairs on the ship."

"But..." Before Taly could ask why that upset them, five chained people were marched into the room surrounded by twenty heavily armed guards, the visors of their helmets pulled down, making them faceless. The guards secured the chains to the floor and then marched out, allowing the first clear look at the prisoners.

Taly's gaze flew over the group. They were all males. Three were cyborgs. Two were not. She felt her heart stop when she realized one of the cyborgs had hair the same color as hers. As the camera traveled over the group, it zoomed in on each face, and her knees gave out. "Ranvir!"

"I know," he told her, holding her upright.

"Loyal citizens of Kirs," Shui's image appeared. It was evident from the throne he sat on that he was on Kirs, not the Nissa. "Before you stand five traitors who have tried to destroy everything we are, everything we stand for. They've already shown how violent they can be.

"How little regard they have for innocent lives by blowing up five ships in their attempt to flee from the sentence they received by the Kirs justice system. Let what happens here today be celebrated throughout our universe, for there will be five fewer traitors for you to worry about. Five less who will murder your children in their sleep. Five less who will threaten our way of life."

Shui looked to his right and nodded.

The transparent wall behind the prisoners began to shimmer, and an unseen wind filled the chamber, lifting the accused off their feet as far as their chains allowed. The cyborgs remained stoic, keeping their arms firmly at their sides as they floated in the air. The other males frantically clawed at their throats, their eyes bulging.

"What... what's going on?" Taly whispered, unable to look away from the horrific scene playing out in front of her. "What's Shui doing to them?"

"He's opening the airlock," Pike told her quietly. "Suffocating them for the entire universe to witness."

The broadcast continued until all five lifeless bodies floated in the room, tethered to this world only by their chains. When the anchors on the floor released, their bodies drifted out into the blackness of space.

"I... I can't believe he did that," she sobbed into Ranvir's chest as Vujcec killed the feed.

"I'm sorry, Taly," Vujcec said quietly. "I would have liked to have met your brother."

"What?" she asked, raising her head to stare at him, confused.

"Your brother, Nas," Vujcec clarified. "I'm sorry he died like that."

"Died like..." Taly shook her head. "None of those cyborgs was Nas."

"What?" Vujcec's eyebrows drew together. "But I thought because of your reaction...."

"It was relief," Ranvir answered for her before looking to the others. "I didn't recognize any of them. Did any of you?"

"No, none of them were from my pod," Pike told him.

"Mine either," Tane said.

"The cyborgs were all from the same pod," Ganesha said quietly. "Their leader was killed when they were originally captured. The other males, I do not know."

"You knew them?" Ranvir asked.

"We were in the same holding cell before Shui's trial," he told them. "They were devastated at their loss and never shared their names."

"We can't let Shui get away with this," Taly said, wiping her cheeks as she stepped away from Ranvir.

"And we won't," Ranvir told her, "but right now, we need to concentrate on what will happen over the next few hours."

Taly sucked in a deep breath and forced herself to calm before nodding. "Of course, which is why I originally came to the bridge. The door to the lower level won't open. Do you know why?"

"Because I secured it," Ranvir told her.

"What? Why?" she demanded.

"Because I wasn't going to allow any of those colonists to wander around the ship. Not when several of them got aggressive with you."

"They were just blowing off steam." She waved a hand dismissively.

"Are you sure about that?" Ranvir asked. "They lost their future and most all their possessions."

"That's my point," she interrupted, but he just continued.

"They know we're cyborgs, Taly. Know they can get credits for turning us in."

"Which is why we should have left them to their fate," Ganesha muttered.

"A fate like the one Shui just gave your fellow cyborgs and innocent civilians?" Taly rounded on the assassin. "Is that what you mean?"

Ganesha had the grace to look ashamed. "No, but they put us at risk."

"Life is a risk. It's how we live it that matters." She let her gaze travel over the room. "And I, for one, am not going to become like Shui and suspect everyone in the universe is against me. Now, I'm going to go check on the colonists, and if I'm not able to," her gaze locked with Ranvir's, "more than the colonists will be getting off on Yelmurn."

With that, she turned and left the bridge.

∞ ∞ ∞ ∞ ∞

"Shit, man, could you have handled that any worse?" Vujcec muttered, glaring at Ranvir.

Ranvir rounded on him. "Shui just executed five innocent people for no reason. Do you know what would happen if he got his hands on Taly?!"

"So you're going to what? Lock her in her stateroom?" Vujcec demanded.

"If I have to," Ranvir admitted.

"And if the ship is boarded, what then? How does she protect herself?" Vujcec watched Ranvir run a frustrated hand through his hair. "Look, I know you're only trying to keep her safe, but Taly knows how to handle herself. Not in combat situations," he admitted, "that's your area, but when it comes to people and working a crowd... there's no one better than Talyani. So let her do what she's good at. Let her feel like she has *some* control in this fucked up situation. That she can contribute."

At their stunned looks, he huffed humorously. "Look, guys, Taly and I know we're the weak links in this group. You can all survive without us, but we can't without you. It's not the most comfortable situation to live in. Knowing you're unnecessary."

"You're not unnecessary, Vujcec," Pike was the first to speak. "You were the one that disarmed the Troubadour's transponder when we forgot to. You were the one who thought to clone the Celerity's code so we could use it."

"You're not a weak link," Tane agreed.

"Neither is Taly," Vujcec told them in a tight voice. "Stop treating her like she is."

Ranvir hated what Vujcec was saying. Hated it because he was right. Taly had more strength and intelligence than any of them gave her credit. All because of her looks and profession. Including him, even after everything she'd done to save them, to get them this far. He didn't include her in his decisions or ask her opinion. That needed to change.

"Tane," he said quietly, "unlock the lower deck."

Chapter Sixteen

Taly still couldn't believe Ranvir had talked to her like that. She wasn't a child. Honestly, she hadn't been one since she won Worlds. She'd dealt with aggressive fans before and knew how to handle them. She also learned how to blend in when she wanted to. All it took was some creative enhancements.

Creative enhancements...

She stored that thought away for later as she approached the door that separated the upper and lower decks of the ship. If it didn't open...

When it whooshed open, she silently thanked the Gods. She didn't like fighting with Ranvir, didn't like fighting with anyone, really, but she wouldn't let him or anyone push her around either.

Heading for the dining room, she found Oved, Sato, and Ree quietly talking as they finished a meal. It seemed the large Madae was always around the couple lately.

"Hello, how are you doing today?" she asked, crossing the room to them.

"Doing very well," Sato told her warmly.

"And Uki here?" She smiled at the baby sleeping contentedly in a woven basket generally used for extra linens.

"She's doing wonderful. She actually slept through the night, which hasn't ever happened before. I always thought she was just hungry." Tears filled her eyes as she looked down at her baby. "Now I think it's because she was in pain and couldn't tell us. We can never thank you enough, Taly."

"No thanks needed. I'm just glad I could help. And speaking of helping, we will be arriving on Yelmurn in a few hours."

"So soon?" Sato murmured, sending a concerned gaze to Oved.

"Yes." Taly's gaze went between the two. "Why? What's wrong?"

"Nothing's wrong," Oved told her, grasping his mate's hand. "It will be fine, Sato."

"But..."

"It will be," he told her firmly. "We have each other and Uki. Nothing else matters."

'Was Ranvir right?' Taly thought. While her life had changed as drastically as these colonists, she wasn't starting over with only the clothes on her back and

a few credits in her pocket. She also had *her* pod, which would hopefully grow when she found Nas.

"I wish there were more I could do," she began.

"Ignore Feo," Oved told her. "You've done more than enough. Thanks to you, we're alive, and our daughter is healthy. We're going to be fine."

"You're right." Sato squeezed his hand. "All we need is each other." She looked to the Madae. "And Ree is planning on traveling with us."

"He is?" Taly sent Ree a questioning look.

"I vowed to see the colonists to Gamma-2, and while I cannot do that for all of them, I can for these three."

"I see," but Taly didn't. Was there something else going on between these three? It was none of her business. "I was hoping I could ask you for some help."

That had them looking at her in confusion. "Us?" Sato asked. "How can we help you?"

"Yes, you see, there are a lot of supplies on the ship that we really don't need. I was hoping you would help me gather and distribute hygiene supplies, bedding, and clothing, so when you all disembark, you at least have something to start with."

"I...that's very generous of you, Taly," Sato said, "and we'd be more than happy to help, and I'm sure others will be, too."

"Great," Taly couldn't help but smile. It felt good to do something that would actually help these people. "Then let's get started."

As they exited the room, Ree pulled her to the side. "What's wrong?" she asked the blue male.

"Don't ignore Feo," he warned. "Or Captain Ju. They are dangerous. If they can harm you, they will."

"Have they said something?" she demanded.

"No, but I know them. Do not stay on Yelmurn any longer than necessary."

∞ ∞ ∞ ∞ ∞

Taly was smiling as she headed back to her suite. They'd been able to find more than she'd expected going through the living quarters of her crew and the storage units. It couldn't replace what the colonists had lost, but at least they would be starting with something.

Ree's warning had her smile dimming. Was he right? Had she underestimated the threat they posed? Should she tell Ranvir about Ree's warning? They were only a few hours out of Yelmurn. Why stir up trouble?

Seeing Vujcec in the hallway, her smile returned. "Are you busy right now?"

"No. I was heading down to get a meal. What do you need?"

"Could you come to my suite for a minute?"

"Ah, sure."

∞ ∞ ∞ ∞ ∞

"Smile," Taly ordered, which Vujcec did. "Now, frown." Again he did as instructed. "It doesn't itch or feel like it's stretching?"

"No. My Gods, I can't believe it." Vujcec touched his face in awe. "How do you know how to do this?"

"I'm an entertainer, Vujcec. To me, using enhancements is what cloning the Celerity's transponder code is to you." She dabbed an application pad into a pot of color that closely resembled Vujcec's natural skin tone, then lightly patted it along the edges of the enhancement she'd applied over Vujcec's brand, blending them in. "There. What do you think?" she asked, stepping back.

"I think it looks amazing." He leaned forward so he was nearly nose to nose with his reflection. "No one would ever suspect I'm a rebel."

"That's the point. Now, remember, don't touch your cheek. It will destroy the effect."

"How long can it stay on?" he asked, still tipping his face up and down, looking at it from various angles.

"It can stay on as long as we're on Yelmurn. After that, it'll need to come off. Otherwise, it could affect your real skin."

Vujcec met her gaze in the mirror. "Will it work on cyborgs?"

"It should. The enhancement will have to be larger, so I'll have to blend more. Also, their nanobots may try to counteract the adhesive, so it may not last as long as yours."

"So we'll have to be quick on Yelmurn."

∞ ∞ ∞ ∞ ∞

Ranvir paused as he walked into the suite, surprised to hear voices coming from the bedroom. He'd known Taly was here. For his peace of mind, he'd had Tane track her the entire time she'd been on the lower deck. He wasn't sure what she'd been doing, going from room to room, but since there had only been two or three people with her at any given time, he hadn't been concerned.

Who was with her? One of the colonists?

They were still a few hours from Yelmurn, and he wanted to apologize to her for how he'd acted on the bridge. For what he'd said. He only wanted to protect her. Surely she'd understand that.

Entering their bedroom, he found Taly and Vujcec exiting the bathroom and drew to a stop. His jaw clenched, and his temper soared. "What the fuck's going on?!"

Taly's eyes widened. Ranvir wanted to kick himself. This was not how he planned to apologize.

"Do you see?" Vujcec ignored Ranvir's outburst as he pointed to his face. "Taly figured out how to temporarily cover our brands."

Ranvir pulled his gaze from Taly's sparking eyes to Vujcec's branded cheek, shocked to see smooth skin. "How?"

"With enhancements, I use when I perform." She lifted the case she carried. "We were just coming to the bridge to work on you guys."

With that, she walked by him and out of the suite. Vujcec gave him a disgusted look as he followed her.

∞ ∞ ∞ ∞ ∞

Ranvir stood by silently and watched Taly work. With an ease of experience, she made Pike's, Tane's, and then Ganesha's brands disappear before wordlessly turning to him. Stepping forward, he took the seat Ganesha vacated, keeping his gaze locked with hers.

He was a cyborg.

That meant he was supposed to be cool, calm, and logical.

He couldn't be with Taly.

"I'm sorry." He didn't try to keep the conversation private. It wouldn't do any good, not with three other cyborgs on the bridge, and Vujcec deserved to hear this. They were his pod now. Whether they decided to create a closed link or not, he would treat them that way. "I should never have spoken to you like that. It was wrong. The only defense I have is that I love you and the thought of
‾ risk makes me act irrationally."

˙ said nothing for a moment. Her cold stare was brutal, and he barely
˥ remain still and hold her gaze.

"Do you think I'm not scared, too?" she finally whispered. "That I don't know it could have been you, any of you caught by Shui and executed?" Her gaze rested for a moment on the other males in the room. "It could have been me. But the only way evil triumphs is when good people do nothing. There are a lot of good people in this universe, Ranvir. We just need to gather them together and fight back."

"You think it's going to be that easy?" Ganesha demanded.

"No." She met Ganesha's gaze straight on. "It's going to be hard. It's going to take time. Lives are going to be lost. Maybe a lot of lives. Shui's insane. He's not going to simply give up. He's going to throw everything he has at us."

Turning, she looked to Pike and Tane. "I know I'm not a cyborg. Or a communications specialist who fought against Shui's evil." She gave Vujcec a small smile. "But I do have access to resources this rebellion will need. Then there's the other important thing I have."

"And what's that?" Ranvir asked.

Turning back to face Ranvir, she gave him a brilliant smile. "My reputation. I'm Talyani. Which, according to Ganesha, makes me Kirs' greatest treasure with supporters that rival Shui's. When I come out on the rebels' side, and we reveal all the atrocities he's committed, we'll have all the supporters we'll need."

"That's not a bad plan," Tane murmured.

"And just so we're clear. I love you too, Ranvir. With all my heart and soul."

Chapter Seventeen

Taly watched as the planet, Yelmurn, grew larger on the bridge's viewing screen as she stood next to Ranvir as he sat in the captain's chair. As it did, so did her nerves. She'd seen visuals of the green planet but had never visited. It was known throughout the system as the garden planet because its moderate climate was perfect for growing a large variety of crops.

"How's the transponder being received?" Ranvir asked, looking to Vujcec from the captain's chair.

"Without a hitch," Vujcec responded from his station. "We've been cleared to land. Quadrant D, Section T-51."

"On the edge of the spaceport. Good. We'll draw less attention there." Ranvir nodded his pleasure.

"I requested one of their prime berths and was informed by a very snooty controller that our hunk of junk would receive the slot it deserved." Vujcec couldn't help but grin.

"Well done," Ranvir told him.

Shifting her weight from foot to foot, Taly stated, "I'll get the credit strips ready. How much do you want on each one?"

"The weapons will be the worst of it," Ranvir said, looking to Pike. "How much did the dealer want?"

"Three," Pike told him. "But you'd better put a little more on it than that. They're likely to raise the price once they're here."

"Three-point five enough?" she asked.

"Make it three point one," Ganesha told her. "I won't let them be that greedy."

Taly could believe that. Who would dare get greedy when dealing with someone who looked like Ganesha? "Same for the power crystals?" she asked.

"Two should be enough for that," Pike answered.

"What about the fuel rods?" Ranvir asked, looking at Tane.

"The spaceport regulates those," Tane responded. "They'll have to be prepaid before delivering to the ship. One should do it."

"A little extra would expedite the process," Pike chimed in.

"I'll put it on a separate strip." Taly gave him a cheeky grin before leaning down to give Ranvir a quick kiss. "Be back in a bit."

∞ ∞ ∞ ∞ ∞

In her suite, Taly went to her personal comm station. Sitting down, she slid her hand under the desk, palm side up, and heard the quiet hum of the scan confirming her identity. Once done, she entered a code, and the entire section retracted into the wall. A new one descended—another one of Nas's recommendations, one he'd personally arranged to have installed.

Opening a drawer, she pulled out blank credit strips and loaded them with credits, making sure there was no way they could be traced to the Troubadour or her. Ranvir would insist on confirming them, but that was fine with her. She'd been transferring credits like this for years. She knew what she was doing.

Finished, she went to shut down the system, then paused and pulled out another strip. After loading it, she secured the system, and the comm station returned to its original state. Watching it, she realized she'd need to show it to Ranvir and add his palmprint so he could access it if he ever needed to.

∞ ∞ ∞ ∞ ∞

"Here are the strips," she announced, returning to the bridge. "Weapons, power crystals, and a little extra." She placed one for each in Ganesha's outstretched hand. "Fuel rods and some for a speedy delivery." She handed those strips to Pike. "And one to send the transmission." She held it up as she moved to where Ranvir stood.

"I would prefer you stay on the ship, but," he quickly added, seeing the thunderous look forming on her face, "I know you won't. So you and I will find a terminal and send your message."

"Thank you." The storm dissipated, and she rose onto her tiptoes and gave him a gentle kiss. He caught her at the waist, keeping her close.

"If I tell you to run, you run," he growled, his arms refusing to release her. "Understand?"

An impish smile crossed her face. "Yes, Ranvir."

"You get your fine ass back to this ship whether I'm with you or not," he continued.

Her smile fell. "But..."

"Swear it! You will not fall into Shui's hands, Talyani. He's not going to do to you what he...."

She cut him off with another kiss, tongue stroking over his until Vujcec cleared his throat, reminding them they weren't alone.

"I swear, Ranvir," she said, breaking off the kiss. Her gaze locked with his, letting him see the truth in hers. "But you'd better get your fine ass back here, too, because I'm coming after you if you don't." She looked to the rest of their group. "And that goes for each and every one of you. We're a *pod*. A *family*. No one gets left behind."

"Yes, Captain." Vujcec snapped to attention, giving her a lousy imitation of a military salute. It was so bad she knew he had to be doing it on purpose to break the tension.

"And don't you forget it," she sassed back, smiling.

A beep had Ganesha turning in his seat. "We'll be entering Yelmurn's atmosphere in five minutes and land in another ten."

"I'll go let the colonists know."

"We'll meet you in the cargo bay once we've landed." Ranvir didn't tell her to be careful again, even though it was on the tip of his tongue. Instead, he'd do what he could to protect her. Looking to Tane, the other cyborg nodded and initiated the tracking beacon on the extraordinary woman they'd all come to care about.

∞ ∞ ∞ ∞ ∞

Taly paused at the door leading to the lower deck. She knew Ranvir had legitimate concerns about her safety with the colonists and on Yelmurn. Even Ree seemed to. But she had just as many about Ranvir's.

She wasn't going to stand out like he did, not with her new haircut and the clothes she wore. No one ever saw her in public when she wasn't projecting her 'Talyani' image. It was a way to keep some semblance of private life. Even when traveling on the Troubadour, she kept up the facade because you never knew who might snap a visual and leak it to the public.

On the other hand, cyborgs tended to move and sound more regimented, especially around other cyborgs. She'd never been sure if it came from being in the military or part of their becoming cyborgs.

Now with Shui's brand on their faces.... But she'd taken care of that. At least temporarily. They'd always have to deal with it like she'd have to deal with being 'Talyani.'

She honestly didn't think the colonists were a danger to her, but she wasn't going to take any chances. Reaching into her pocket, she touched the mini blaster she kept in her suite. It was currently set to stun but could kill if necessary. It was yet another thing Nas had insisted on, for which she was grateful.

She silently prayed she wouldn't need it. Stepping forward, the door opened to the lower level.

∞ ∞ ∞ ∞ ∞

She found the colonists waiting in the dining room, all clutching baskets filled with the supplies Oved, Sato, and Ree had helped her gather and distribute. "We'll be landing on Yelmurn in about ten minutes. Do you have everything you need?"

"What we need is to be taken to Gamma-2," a familiar voice yelled.

"Which isn't going to happen." Taly's gaze locked with Feo's, standing in the back. She reached into her pocket as his muscles bulged and his face reddened.

Captain Ju whispered something in Feo's ear, and he finally looked away. She wouldn't be sorry to see the last of those two.

"We're ready, Taly." Sato moved toward Taly with Uki strapped to her chest, Oved and Ree close behind, each carrying a large bundle of supplies on their backs.

Taly gave them a small smile. These four she'd miss. "Then let's get down to the cargo bay."

Turning, she led the way.

∞ ∞ ∞ ∞ ∞

Ranvir looked to Pike as the Troubadour touched down on their designated landing area. "Contact your dealer. I want the weapons and crystals here within the hour. Vujcec, you'll stay here and assist Ganesha. Tane, you go with Pike. I want this operation quick and clean.

"The sooner we're off this rock, the sooner we can take the fight to Shui. Vujcec, all comms on an encrypted channel now. I want to be kept informed on every step of this op. Understood?"

He looked at each pod member, and for the first time since being captured, he felt like he was back doing what he did best—leading an op.

"Understood, Major," their firm replies filled the room.

"Then let's do this."

∞ ∞ ∞ ∞ ∞

Taly's eyes widened as Ranvir entered the cargo bay, followed by the rest of their pod. They stood shoulder-to-shoulder, looking fierce while forming an impenetrable wall.

This version of Ranvir wasn't the warm, gentle male she'd come to know and love. No, now he was the cold, calculating cyborg he'd been trained to be. His gaze slowly traveled over each person there as if committing their faces to memory. It had many of the colonists moving closer to the outer door.

"We saved you from certain death. Brought you to a place where you have a chance to move on with your lives. Repay that kindness with betrayal, and I will personally hunt each and every one of you down. I will end your life and the life of every member of your family. Painfully." With that announcement out of the way, Ranvir grabbed the release lever for the outer door.

Taly watched the colonists trip over themselves to get off the Troubadour as if the Gods of hell themselves were after them. Maybe they were. She grabbed Sato's arm before she followed.

"Here." She slipped the extra credit strip into Sato's hand. "It's not much, but it should get you and your family to Gamma-2."

Sato's hand closed around the strip as she pulled Taly in for a one-armed hug. "Thank you, Taly. For everything. We'll never forget you." With that, they were gone.

Ranvir didn't say anything. It was one of the things he loved about Taly. She wasn't naive. She couldn't have gotten to where she was if she had been, but she hadn't let it harden her. She couldn't help everyone, but that didn't stop her from doing what she could.

He took the grey cape Vujcec carried, put it around her shoulders, and then pulled one on himself. She eyed him questioningly. "It will help us blend in and cover the bulge of that blaster you have in your pocket."

She smiled at that. "Noticed that, did you?"

"I notice everything when it comes to you." He handed her an ear comm. She shouldn't need it since he wasn't leaving her side, but he wasn't taking any chances. "It's programmed with an encrypted channel."

"All right," she said, putting the device in her ear.

"You will do exactly what I say," he reminded her. "You will not leave my side."

"I will, and I won't." Rising up on her toes, she gave him a quick kiss. "Don't worry. Everything will be fine."

Chapter Eighteen

The first impression of Yelmurn shocked Taly. From space, the planet looked like a green jewel. Stepping onto it, she discovered only brown lifelessness.

"It's a spaceport," Ranvir said quietly, knowing what she was thinking. "This area is where the less 'attractive' ships are berthed."

Taly turned and looked at the Troubadour with its long sleek lines and reflective surface.

"She stands out like a power crystal in space," Ranvir agreed as he pulled her hood up to cover her hair. The cape shielded the majority of her face while allowing her to see. "Which is why we need to hurry before the tower realizes she's not the Celerity."

Pulling up his hood, he guided her across the tarmac and into the city's dusty streets surrounding it. Moving quickly, his eyes continually scanned for threats.

Yelmurn was mainly a peaceful agricultural planet, but every planet had its dark underbelly, which is why the Cyborg Elite were here. As they moved deeper into the city, the streets changed from dirt to stone, which widened into its central market.

Taly gasped, taking in the scene before her. The market was filled with colorful stalls set close together, so customers had to follow designated paths. Each stall had pendants flying from the point of their roofs, listing the goods they sold.

It was a symphony of sights, sounds, and smells that had Taly smiling from ear to ear. She loved places like this. They fed her creativity, so she made a point of visiting them on all her tour stops.

Ranvir's grip tightened on her arm when she paused at a stall full of beautiful scarves. She looked up.

"We don't have time for that," he murmured, pulling her away before the owner noticed her interest.

She knew that was true. Still, she couldn't resist one last look at the stall. As Ranvir led her deeper into the market, a vendor would occasionally step in front of them in an attempt to stop them and hawk their wares. It only took a glance from Ranvir for them to quickly realize their mistake and scurry away.

"There." Ranvir gestured down the path with his chin to a stall with a banner proclaiming it had an intergalactic link.

Taly took in the cafe with its bright blue and white panels extended out to provide shade for its customers sitting outside at little tables and was delighted. "Oh, it's charming, and look, it says they have homemade buns." She clapped her hands together. "We have to try them."

"We don't have time for food," he told her gruffly.

"But..."

"No, Taly. We're risking enough just being here," he reminded her, his gaze scanning for threats. "We send the message, then get back to the ship."

For a moment, she'd forgotten the danger they were in.

"Welcome," a blue-skinned female greeted with a beaming smile, "I'm Vanni. It's a beautiful day. Would you like to sit on our patio?"

"We need a comm station," Ranvir told her abruptly. "One with an intergalactic link."

"Of course." The greeter's smile dimmed at his gruffness. "Right this way."

Ranvir silently followed behind Taly as they were led to a station near the back of the cafe. He noted who looked up as they passed and who ignored them.

"This is perfect," Taly told the female. "Thank you."

"Your server..."

"We don't need one." Ranvir cut her off, his hard look causing her to bump into another table as she hurried away.

"That wasn't necessary," Taly murmured as she sat down at the surprisingly clean station.

"We're not here to make friends," he told her.

"We're not here to make enemies either. We have enough of them." Sliding the credit strip into its slot, she waited for the system to boot up. Once it did, she entered the channel and destination for her message on the keyboard. When it was verified, she approved the transfer of credits from the credit strip and began typing her message.

'Hi, big brother. I hope you are well with everything that's happening right now. I'd love to talk with you and catch up. Call HOME when you can. Love you, your little sis.'

Taly wanted to add more and let Nas know she was okay and who she was with, but Nas had insisted they keep their messages short. They needed to reveal no pertinent information. Knowing she'd said all she could, she hit send.

Ranvir stood with his back to Taly, blocking her from the curious eyes she was drawing as he scanned the room. The cafe was only partially full, and while several patrons were openly curious, he doubted the youngsters posed any real threat.

The male outside across the path, trying to look casual, had all Ranvir's systems going on alert, though. He was a scrawny male, but his gaze never left the cafe, and he repeatedly reached up to touch his ear comm. That told Ranvir he was a scout, not a fighter. It was time to go.

"Done." Taly pulled the credit strip from the terminal. She stood, and Ranvir adjusted her hood, ensuring it still obscured her face before gripping her arm and silently leading her outside.

"What's wrong?" she asked once they were away from the cafe.

His pace quickened. "We're being followed."

"What?!"

When she attempted to spin around, his grip tightened on her arm. "Don't. Keep moving."

He hurried them down one path and then another before pulling her into a small gap between two stalls. Moments later, the scout hurried past. Once he was out of sight, Ranvir pulled Taly back the way they'd come.

He touched his ear comm and demanded, "Report."

"Weapons arriving now," Ganesha answered.

"Fuel rods in transit," Pike added.

"Stay alert. We had to lose a scout." He heard them both curse. "The transmission has been sent. We're on our way back. Contact me immediately if there's any trouble."

Once he ended the comm, Taly asked, "Is everyone all right?"

"For now. We need to get back to the ship." They'd nearly made it out of the market when Oved and Sato came running up to them, Uki strapped to Sato's chest. Ree following close behind, his blaster out.

"You have to hide," Oved told them, frantically looking behind them. "Bounty hunters are heading this way."

"You turned us in!" Ranvir lunged for Oved only to have Ree step between them.

"It wasn't us," Ree told him chest-to-chest with Ranvir.

"It wasn't!" Sato added her voice to Ree's. "It was Ju and Feo. We overheard them in the market and were heading back to the ship to warn you when we saw you!"

"They wouldn't do that, Ranvir?" Taly gripped his arm and pulled him away from Ree. When he turned, she let out a small gasp. "Ranvir," she whispered, "your brand is showing."

She'd obviously misjudged how long the enhancement would hold up against a cyborg's nanobots.

A crowd gathered behind them—the words 'cyborg' and 'rebel' began spreading like wildfire.

"There's one!" someone shouted from behind the crowd. "Get him!"

Ranvir's eyes locked with Ree's. "Get them back to the ship!" he ordered, whipping off his cape and launching himself into the crowd.

"Ranvir!" Taly froze, unable to believe the number of people that had engulfed him. She had promised Ranvir she would run if he said so, but she'd never actually believed it would come to that.

"Come on, Taly." Ree pulled her away with his blaster free hand. "You can't help him. You'll only be in the way."

Taly looked behind her one last time. Ranvir disappeared from view within the angry, yelling mob. Heart in her throat, she turned and ran after Sato and her family out of the market, with Ree bringing up the rear.

∞ ∞ ∞ ∞ ∞

The crowd didn't concern Ranvir. None were equipped to take on a cyborg. His concern was on Taly. He'd seen her hesitation in leaving him and was grateful that Ree had convinced her to go. He couldn't fight the way he needed to and protect her simultaneously.

He tossed idiots in the air one after the other and touched his ear comm.

"Ganesha."

"We've been betrayed," he spat.

The crowd parted, and three bounty hunters stepped forward, blasters drawn. Captain Ju and Feo stood close behind them.

"Who?" Ganesha demanded.

"Ju and Feo," Ranvir told him, pulling his own blaster. The odds were against him, but he had to give Taly as much time as possible to get away. "Taly is on her way back to you with some colonists that warned us. Make sure she gets there."

"We will, then we'll come for you."

"Forget about me," Ranvir said. He dove for cover as all three bounty hunters opened fire on him. "If I'm not there when you have Taly secured, take off without me."

Rising to his feet, he fired and ran in the direction Taly had taken. He didn't need to verify his aim had been true. He never missed at that range.

He ducked between shadowy doorways. Two bounty hunters slowly crept down the street while Ju and Feo remained near its entrance. Obviously, they believed they were safe there. They weren't. Ranvir had warned them on the ship what would happen if they betrayed them.

Lifting his blaster, he stepped out of the doorway and sent off two quick bursts. As they returned fire, the bounty hunters dove for cover, but Ranvir was already running farther down the street. Ju and Feo fell backward to the ground, sizzling holes at the center of their foreheads right between their eyes.

Ranvir cursed when he felt a searing pain in his leg. Stumbling, he dove into another doorway. He didn't bother glancing down at the wound. He'd been grazed by one of the bounty hunters. His cybernetic processors were already analyzing and sending the necessary nanobots to repair the injury.

He should have stayed focused on the bounty hunters and ignored Ju and Feo. Still, it felt good knowing those two fuckers were dead.

Sticking his head out, he quickly located one of the bounty hunters slowly moving toward him. Ranvir fired.

Then there was one.

"Taly is on board," came over Ranvir's ear comm. In the background, Taly yelled over Ganesha's comm.

"Problems?" Ranvir asked, fearing something had happened to her.

"Only with your cymar," he heard Ganesha grunt. "What's your status?"

"One target remaining."

"Take him out and get back here. We're starting to draw attention."

"Take off without me." Ranvir closed the comm but not before hearing Taly's scream of denial. Taking a deep breath, he moved out of the doorway and rushed his remaining target.

Chapter Nineteen

Taly's mind raced as fast as her feet moved. She couldn't believe this. They'd saved Ju and Feo's lives. For them to betray them like this... She should have listened to Ranvir about assisting the Celerity. She should have told him what Ree had said. If she had, they wouldn't be in this situation.

Except... her gaze locked with Uki's big brown eyes, protectively strapped to her mother's chest. If she'd listened to Ranvir, this precious little one would be no more. So she had to believe she'd done the right thing. There was a reason this was happening.

The buildings fell away behind them while they ran, Taly's thoughts on Ranvir. He had to be okay. He would be catching up with them soon. Reaching the spaceport, Ganesha and Tane rushed toward them, blasters drawn.

"Ranvir is still back there," she told Ganesha as he herded them across the tarmac toward the ramp Pike and Wells were guarding.

The giant cyborg said nothing until he had her on board. "We know," he finally told her.

"Then go help him," she demanded.

"He ordered us to secure you and remain here." He touched his ear comm. "Taly's on board."

"I don't care what he said!" Taly argued, moving back toward the ramp only to have him block her. She threw an elbow into his stomach, hoping to get around him, but he easily fended her efforts and continued his conversation with Ranvir.

"Only with your cymar. What's your status?"

Touching her own ear comm, she heard Ranvir order, "Take off."

"No!" she screamed.

This time she got around Ganesha. She ran for the exit, but Pike stepped into her path. She shoved at him and received a grunt for her efforts, but he didn't move.

"Get out of my way," she ordered. "We're not leaving him."

"We're not," Pike told her. "But we have to ensure the ship is ready to take off as soon as he gets here. We can't do that if we're chasing after you."

"Swear it," she demanded.

"I swear," he immediately responded. "We don't leave pod members behind."

Taly looked to Ganesha, and he agreed, "We don't."

Taking a deep breath, she nodded. "Okay. What do you need me to do?"

∞ ∞ ∞ ∞ ∞

Ranvir limped down the street, pissed at the fact the last bounty hunter got off a shot before Ranvir could finish him. His nanobots rushed to repair the damage on top of the prior injury, but he didn't have the time to stand around and wait to heal.

Not if he wanted to get off this planet alive. He needed to get to the Troubadour if it was still there.

"Ganesha," he said after activating his ear comm. If he didn't reply, he had followed Ranvir's orders, and he'd have to find another way off this planet.

"About fucking time," Ganesha responded.

"All threats neutralized. I'm five minutes out."

"Make it two. Port security will be here in three."

"Leave me."

"Can't."

"That's an order, Cyborg."

"You've been overruled by the captain... and the rest of our pod."

This time when Ranvir stumbled, it had nothing to do with his injury. He hadn't expected this. He'd brought up forming a new pod, but nothing had been decided. For Ganesha to word it that way meant it had.

"Taly's the priority," he said instead.

"We're not leaving without you, Ranvir, so get your ass in gear or so help the Gods, I'm coming out there and getting you myself." Taly's beautiful voice filled his ear. The harsh tone left no doubt about how upset she was with him.

"Don't you dare!" he growled and pushed his leg to its limits. He had to hurry because he didn't doubt for one nanosecond that she didn't mean the threat. There was no way he'd chance her getting off the Troubadour. "Ganesha. Status."

"Ship is secure. Engines are primed. All we're waiting on is you."

"Nearly there," he said as he burst onto the tarmac.

The Troubadour sat before him. Systems lit as proof she was ready to take off. Several guards surrounded the vessel. The ramp wasn't out, preventing the security forces from gaining entry. The hatch had been left open, and he could see Pike standing in it.

The moment Pike spotted Ranvir, he raised his blaster and began laying cover fire. The security force dove for cover, clearing a direct path for Ranvir to the ship.

As he leaped for the hatch, his injured leg gave out. Adrenaline surged through his systems. He was going to miss the opening completely. Suddenly, Pike dropped his blaster and reached down. Rough hands grabbed Ranvir's forearms and swung him into the ship. They both fell backward onto the deck.

"He's on board!" Pike yelled, hitting his ear comm. "Close the hatch and get us out of here."

In an instant, the hatch closed, and the ship wobbled beneath him as it lifted off.

"Thanks," he told Pike as he gingerly rolled to his feet.

Pike was up faster, his gaze going to Ranvir's pant leg soaked with blood. "We need to get you to medical."

"I'm fine," Ranvir told him.

"Right," Pike huffed. "That's why you couldn't make a jump a day-old cyborg could."

Ranvir looked at his leg and grimaced. "The second hit did more damage than I thought."

"Second?" Pike questioned.

"Yeah. For bounty hunters, they were pretty good shots."

"What about Ju and Feo?" Pike demanded.

"Dead."

They both reached out to steady themselves as the ship tilted onto its side.

"What's going on up there?" Ranvir demanded through his ear comm.

"If you want to know, get your lazy asses up here and find out." Ganesha's tense reply had them hustling for the bridge.

∞ ∞ ∞ ∞ ∞

"Strap your ass into the captain's chair and stay there," Ganesha ordered Taly as he did the same in the pilot's chair.

"But..."

"He's close," Ganesha told her. "As soon as he's in, we need to take off. Fast."

Taly looked to the people that had risked their lives to save her and Ranvir. She'd refused to leave them behind. It hadn't taken much convincing on her part. Not with all the blaster fire.

"There are seats along that wall for you," she pointed to them. "Get strapped in. I have a feeling this is going to get bumpy."

"There he is."

Tane's comment had Taly's gaze swinging back to the main screen. Ranvir sprinted across the tarmac, favoring his right leg, blaster fire surrounding him.

"They're firing on him!" she exclaimed.

"No, we are, to clear a path. Now strap in!" Ganesha ordered again.

As she took the captain's chair and secured her harness, Pike's voice yelled over her ear comm. "He's on board. Close the hatch and get us out of here."

The next moment, the ship lifted off, and she fell back in her seat at the sharp angle used for their ascent.

"Celerity, you have not been cleared for takeoff. Return to Quadrant D, Section T-51 immediately."

The announcement blared over the intercom.

"Sure. We'll get right on that," Vujcec muttered before ending the transmission.

"Hang on," Ganesha ordered moments before the ship rocked hard to the left.

"What's going on up there?" Ranvir snapped.

"If you want to know, get your lazy asses up here and find out," Ganesha replied tersely, making several more sharp maneuvers before breaking out of Yelmurn's atmosphere.

"What the hell's going on?!" Ranvir demanded as he and Pike stormed onto the bridge.

"Apparently, the bounty hunters chasing you had friends. Friends with ships." Ganesha glanced at Tane. "How many are still chasing us?"

"Just one, but we're already out of weapons range," Tane told him.

"They fired on us?" Ranvir hadn't heard any hits.

"No," Tane told him. "I scanned those in pursuit, and none had atmospheric weapons. Our rear shields are back to full power even if they did."

"You were able to install the crystals?" Ranvir was impressed. He knew it took a skilled hand to do that under the best conditions.

"With Vujcec's help, yes," Pike told him. "We decided the shields were the priority."

"Good call," Ranvir praised. "We need shields more than weapons and fuel rods. They are all within acceptable levels. Have we lost the last ship?"

"Yes," Tane told him. "Gods, this baby's fast."

"Especially in the hands of a skilled pilot," Ranvir added.

It may have seemed a casual observance to a non-cyborg, but it was the greatest of compliments, and they knew it.

"You're hurt." Taly jumped from the captain's chair and dropped to her knees beside Ranvir. Tearing the hole in his pants wider, she gasped. "We need to get you to medical."

"My nanobots are already repairing the damage from both injuries," he assured her as he reached down and helped her back to her feet.

"Both?!" Her fingers dug into his arm.

"He was hit twice," Pike told her, ignoring Ranvir's glare.

"Then you're definitely going to medical," she told him.

A small cry had them turning to the passengers they'd forgotten about.

"What are they doing here?" Ranvir demanded.

"I wasn't going to leave them on Yelmurn," Taly told him stubbornly. "Not after they warned us about Ju and Feo."

Ranvir tipped his head back toward the ceiling with a groan. How could he forget how soft-hearted Taly was? The Madae had already proven to be an asset. He had a cool head and could handle himself. Something he couldn't say when it came to the family. Still, they had come to their aid. His gut warned this wasn't a good idea. Being on this ship was dangerous.

"I can pilot any ship, am skilled with a blaster, and an expert in hand-to-hand combat." Ree listed off his assets.

Understanding what Ree was doing, Oved began pleading their case "We won't be a burden. My Sato is an amazing cook, and I know my way around machines."

He suddenly realized how that must have sounded at the hard looks he received in return, including from his wife. "No! I'm not talking about you. I don't consider you machines. I meant the engines! Or anything else mechanical. I can fix anything."

"He really can." Sato earnestly supported her husband. "He's a genius. It's why we were going to Gamma-2. They need mechanics."

"I know you didn't mean it that way, Oved. And I'm sure everyone else does, too. Right guys?" Taly gave each cyborg a pointed look. "Right?"

"Right," three of them agreed.

"Ganesha?" she asked the only cyborg who didn't respond.

"Sure," he finally said before swinging back around to face forward.

Taly would have liked a better response from them but didn't want to push it. "Great. Sato, why don't you guys go down to the lower level? You can pick what quarters you want and get something to eat if you're hungry while I take Ranvir to medical."

Her gaze shot back to Ranvir. He'd opened his mouth to argue but snapped it shut at her glare.

∞ ∞ ∞ ∞ ∞

Ranvir lay on the med bed, letting it scan him to ease Taly's mind. "The readout says your leg is nearly healed, but your nanobot levels need replenishing."

"Wait!"

He was too late. A pressure syringe was lowered to his neck and injected him with lifesaving little machines. Kirs' scientists were always making what they considered 'advancements' in the nanobots, unconcerned with how they might interact with what was currently in a cyborg's system, which was why new infusions were only done in extreme circumstances.

Taly hadn't given him a chance to warn her. Gritting his teeth in dread, he waited for the sting as the two different nanobots fought for dominance. When several moments passed, and nothing happened, he tipped his head back to see Taly still at the control panel.

"Why doesn't it hurt?" he asked.

She frowned. "Hurt? It shouldn't. This bed identifies your specific nanobots and programs the new ones to be compatible."

He'd never heard of such a thing. "That's possible?"

"It is now."

Ranvir shook his head in disbelief and relaxed. His processors confirmed Taly's statement. With the influx of more nanobots, his injury finished repairing in record time.

Once the bed shut down, he sat up and swung his legs over the edge. "Thank you, Taly. That really helped."

She smirked. "Even though you didn't want or think it was necessary?"

"That's true. I didn't know this was possible. Cyborgs have been severely damaged when too many of their original nanobots remain when infused with new ones. They sometimes see the original nanobots as a parasite to be eradicated."

Her mouth dropped. "You thought I would inject you without knowing that?"

He ran his hand roughly down his face.

"Do you really think I would take that chance without knowing it was perfectly safe for you?" Taly continued.

Hurt at his lack of faith in her, she headed for the door. Tears blurred her vision, and she ran into an immovable object. Blinking, she glanced up at the hard chest in front of her.

"I'm sorry," Ranvir murmured, wrapping his arms around. She remained still in his embrace. "I know you would never intentionally harm me. There is a lot of information about cyborgs that isn't common knowledge, not even among cyborgs. I reacted instinctively."

She softened and leaned into his weight. "I should have explained first and given you a choice instead of injecting you without permission."

He ran his hands up her back and down again, soothing the tense line of her spine. "It seems we're both used to doing instead of asking. We'll each have to work on that."

She nodded and rested her head against his chest. "I guess we will. So is your leg feeling better?"

She let out a little shriek when he swung her up into his arms.

"I'll prove it to you."

Chapter Twenty

Taly's laughter filled the upper corridor. "Ranvir. What are you doing?"

"Showing you how fully recovered I am," he told her, entering their quarters.

"Well, in that case." Twisting in his arms, she wrapped her arms and legs around him, pulled his head down, and captured his lips for a deep, hard kiss.

Ranvir came to an abrupt halt, realizing they weren't going to make it to the bed. Spinning, he pressed her against the wall and hungrily returned her kiss. He gave little thought to her clothing as his hands tore them away. He needed her. Needed to be inside her.

He could have lost her today. He'd seen her hesitate when he'd told her to run. If that mob had gone after her instead of him, he would have turned into that ruthless, emotionless killing machine, so many thought cyborgs were. It was something they would be having a long discussion about. Later. Right now, he needed to prove that they were both alive and whole.

Ripping his mouth from hers, he hoisted her up higher on the wall, his mouth blazing a trail along her jaw and neck, sucking and nipping his way down until he reached the valley between her now bare breasts. He captured first one already pebbled peak in his mouth and then the other, causing her to cry out.

"Ranvir!" Her fingers dug into his shoulders as he released one nipple with a pop.

He knew he needed to slow down, but not even his processors could control the desire and need flooding him. With her back braced against the wall, his thumb glided through her damp curls until it reached her clit.

Rubbing it, he got the response he wanted as his cymar rocked her hips, seeking more of his touch. He gave it to her, driving her desire higher and higher until she cried out with need.

Gripping the fastener of his pants, he released his aching cock and placed it at her dripping opening.

"Ready for me?" he asked, lifting his head to take in her swollen lips, flushed face, and passion-dazed eyes.

"Gods, yes," she panted.

Needing no further reassurance, he gripped her hips and impaled her on his cock with one hard thrust. The feel of her hot silky depths enveloping him snapped what little control he had left.

His breath quickened as he plunged into her harder and faster until he thought his heart would burst. She matched him thrust for thrust, her fingers digging into his biceps. He felt her muscles fist around him and emptied himself into her with one final thrust.

∞ ∞ ∞ ∞ ∞

Taly lay across Ranvir's chest on the couch and tried to catch her breath. She wasn't sure how they'd gotten there but didn't care. All she cared about was that Ranvir was in her arms, whole and alive.

She'd never been so scared as she'd been watching Ranvir take on that mob alone. She'd always known life was precarious, but that had brought it into sharp focus. Now, she would savor every moment she had with Ranvir because it might be their last.

"What has you thinking so hard?" Ranvir asked as the fingers of one hand lazily ran up and down her back.

"How close I came to losing you today," she murmured.

"I'm hard to kill, Taly."

She rose up on an elbow, her head resting in her palm to gaze down at him. "So were those cyborgs Shui executed. If that had been you...."

"I don't know how those cyborgs were captured, but I do know that they didn't have someone like you there to assist them. If they had, they'd still be alive."

Taly felt her eyes begin to fill. This all started because she wanted to save one cyborg, her brother. Now, she wanted to do more than that. She wanted to save all of them, their families, and anyone else willing to stand up against Shui.

She just wished she knew how to do that.

"Hey." Reaching up, he gently cupped her jaw using his thumb to wipe away a tear. "It's going to be okay."

"Is it?" Her eyes searched his. "You were shot, Ranvir. Twice. If those bounty hunters had better aim, we wouldn't be having this conversation."

She could see he wanted to argue with her, but cyborgs didn't lie. Sighing, she laid her head on his chest and let the beat of his heart soothe her.

"What are we going to do now, Ranvir?"

"Wait for Nas to respond to your message."

"And if he doesn't?" she voiced her fear.

"He will. Did Nas ever tell you what happens when a member dies in a pod?"

Her gaze shot to his. "No."

"It's instantly felt throughout the pod." His eyes became distant as if he were remembering something painful. "It can be crippling."

"You've experienced this?" she murmured.

"Yes." He seemed to pull himself out of the past and focused on her. "I've lost two pod members since becoming a cyborg. Once when I served under Nas. The other when commanding my own pod. Both were like losing a brother."

"I'm sorry." Reaching up, she caressed his cheek.

"Thank you, but I'm telling you this because I haven't experienced that loss for Nas."

Hope filled her only to fade away when she remembered. "But you aren't a member of Nas's pod anymore."

"True, but he and I never severed our link. We'd served together for too long."

"So you're saying," hope bloomed inside her again, "you would know if Nas were dead?"

"Yes."

The sob burst from her, and she buried her face in his chest. Gods, she'd never admitted, even to herself, the chance that her brother was dead.

"Shh, it's okay." His arms tightened around her, pulling her close.

"I've been imagining so many terrible things since that execution." She knew she could admit that to him.

"I'm sorry I didn't mention the link sooner. I assumed with everything Nas told you about us, he would have revealed that."

"Nas only tells you what he wants you to know," she huffed out humorlessly.

"Isn't that the truth," Ranvir agreed. "In all these years, he never said a word about you."

"He takes being the protective older brother seriously." She smiled up at him even though her cheeks were still wet.

"Nas takes everything seriously," Ranvir smiled down at her. "He always had a backup plan for his backup plan."

"I can believe that. Although I doubt even Nas could have prepared for what Shui did."

"I wouldn't be too sure of that. After all, he advised you to get this ship."

"And arranged to have it outfitted with a few extras. Which reminds me." Rising from the couch, she walked over to her comm station, unconcerned about her nudity.

Ranvir frowned but rose and followed her. "You mean there's more than I've already seen?"

"Yes."

He watched her sit down and then heard the hum when she slid her hand under the desk, palm side up. "Your comm station is palm coded?"

She smiled over her shoulder at him. "It is, and we need to get it to recognize yours, but first." She entered a code, and the entire wall section retracted, and a new station descended.

"Gods almighty!" Ranvir swore, his gaze rapidly moving over the sleek station. "Do you know what this is?"

"A top-of-the-line comm station?" she asked, carefully glancing up at him.

"It's more than that. It's a stealth system." He gave her a hard look. "This is how you accessed your credits, isn't it? Where you filled those credit strips."

"Yes. It's linked to all my hidden accounts. It's also what I use when I talk to Nas. Everything is fully encrypted." She entered a code, and the panel beneath the station glowed red. "Put your palm on it so I can give you access to the system."

Once he did, the system hummed until the panel turned green.

"There we go," she entered a few more codes, "now you have access to everything."

"I can't believe you did that," he said quietly.

"Did what?" She looked up at him in confusion.

"You just gave me access to all your accounts," he told her, his disbelief easily heard.

"Why wouldn't I?" she asked. "I love you, and besides, someone other than me needs to know how to access them."

"Nas doesn't know how?"

"He does. After all, he helped me set them up, but he's never accessed them." Her eyes widened. "But he would if he needed credits." She spun back to the station and began to furiously type, checking first one account and then another until her shoulders sagged in defeat. "He hasn't accessed any of the accounts."

Dropping to his knees, he ran a reassuring hand along her leg. "He wouldn't, Taly. Not if there was the slightest chance of the transmission being intercepted. He wouldn't risk you that way."

"I'd just hoped...."

"I know, but he will contact us."

The ringing of the comm had them both looking to the station. Ranvir was the one that answered.

"What is it?"

"Major," Vujcec's voice came through the earbuds they still wore. "There's a transmission you and Taly will want to see."

"On our way."

∞ ∞ ∞ ∞ ∞

Taly stared at the view screen in disbelief. Some enterprising being had recorded the entire incident on the tarmac of Yelmurn. Not only had they captured it, but they'd also somehow been able to recognize Talyani.

The angle zoomed-in when her hood fell back as she struggled against two large men. Ganesha and Pike prevented her from getting off the ship to help Ranvir.

The narrator claimed they were restraining her. They were abducting her to do unspeakable things to her. They were ruthless cyborgs, after all.

No one could refute the claim to their identities after seeing Ranvir make the impossible leap from the deck into the ship's hatch several meters high.

The narrator demanded the authorities should come to her aid, even though he'd stood by and done nothing.

"Gods damned, fucking shit!" Taly ignored the shocked looks she received for her extreme profanity. "How the fuck were they able to get this out so fast?"

"You're Talyani," Vujcec said as if that answered everything.

"They also revealed our transponder code," Tane told them. "The entire universe will now be looking for it."

"Shut it down, Vujcec," Ranvir ordered.

"Already done," he replied.

"Now we need to decide what to do," Ranvir told them. "Especially with innocent civilians on board."

Taly walked over to Vujcec's comm center and pressed a button. "Oved. Sato. Ree. Could you return to the bridge, please?"

"What are you doing, Taly?" Ranvir asked.

"It's not our place to decide their future," she said.

"And if they choose to turn us in?" Ganesha questioned.

"If they'd wanted to do that, they wouldn't have helped us on Yelmurn. It's only right they are included in this." She looked to Vujcec. "What has been the response to the recording on social media?"

"Shock. Disbelief. Mistrust," Vujcec told her. "Many are claiming it's a hoax."

"What is it, Taly?" Oved asked as they hurried onto the bridge.

"Replay the recording, Vujcec," Taly ordered.

"Dear Gods in the heavens," Sato whispered. "Oved, we can be identified from that."

"It will be fine, Sato." Oved pulled his wife close, trying to reassure her, but Taly could see the fear in his eyes.

"It's why we wanted you here," Ranvir told them. "Your faces are now forever linked with ours. People are going to be looking for you as wanted criminals. You are welcome to stay with us, but we can't guarantee your safety. Or we can drop you off somewhere, and you can take your chances on your own."

Silence reigned as the two looked from each other to Uki, sleeping innocently against her mother's chest. Finally, they looked to Taly, a decision made without exchanging a word.

"We will stay with you and help you fight against Emperor Shui," Oved told them.

"How do you know that's what we plan on doing?!" Ranvir demanded.

Taly's hand on his arm stopped him from advancing.

"Because you are cyborgs," Oved replied, unfazed by Ranvir's move. "It is what you've sworn to do. To protect our people from any force that would try and destroy them. Which is what Shui is doing. Destroying our people by murdering anyone who speaks out against him." Oved looked down at his

Uki. "My daughter will not grow up in a world like that. Not when I can do something to help prevent it."

"*We* can," Sato added her voice to his. "Whatever we can do to assist you, we will."

"I will also assist you," Ree told them quietly, but his eyes sparked with rage. "What was done to you is wrong. Justice must be found."

Silence filled the bridge. Civilians usually saw cyborgs only as a necessary evil, one barely tolerated. For these three to support them and believe in them was shocking.

"Thank you, Oved. Sato. Ree. Welcome to our pod." Taly turned to the rest of their pod. "So, what's our next move?"

∞ ∞ ∞ ∞ ∞

"I don't like it," Ranvir repeated his objection.

"It has to be done at some point, Ranvir," Taly reminded him as she carefully applied her enhancements. "Now is the perfect time when everyone has watched that recording."

"We need to be further away from Yelmurn." He watched what she was doing in the mirror.

"Then we'll be out of range of the relay station Vujcec was able to tap into. Relax, Ranvir." Her gaze met his in the mirror. "I can handle this."

"It will put a target on your back." The thought of her in danger drove him crazy.

"It's already there, and we both know it," she countered. "If Shui somehow manages to kill me before I speak out, he'll be able to blame the rebels."

He spun her around in her chair. He yanked her up. "You think I can't protect you?"

Her eyes widened for a moment, then she reached up and cupped his face between her hands. "I know you will protect me with your last breath, but we both know nothing is certain in life. Nothing but my love for you. I'm not going to allow Shui to use me against you, against Nas, against those who are only trying to protect the people on Kirs."

"What about your parents?" He didn't want to hurt her, but he had to make sure she understood that it couldn't be undone once she did this.

Taly's eyes filled, but she refused to let the tears fall. Her parents may not have known what Shui had planned, but they weren't innocent in what had happened. They'd chosen to support the emperor. Now they'd have to live with that choice. And possibly die because of it.

"They chose their side." Taking a step back, she asked. "How do I look?"

It was something she'd given great thought. She'd done hundreds, thousands of interviews and social media spots. In all of them, she presented what people expected to see. An entertainer. A star. Someone they wanted her to be.

Today she needed them to see her as a citizen—one they recognized and trusted but who was just like them.

Ranvir let his gaze travel over her. She was still his Taly, but right now, she was more. Since the recording revealed her short blonde locks, she'd made no attempt to conceal them.

Instead, she'd enhanced them, making them fuller and shinier but still natural-looking. She'd also spent time on her face. Her lips were fuller but contained no artificial color. She'd outlined her eyes but had added no other enhancements.

The outfit she wore was form-fitting but not glitzy or sparkly. She'd found a pair of multi-pocket black pants, a short-sleeved black pullover, and low-heeled black boots nearly identical to an Elite military uniform. She could easily pass for a cyborg.

When Ranvir remained silent, she gave him an uncertain look. "Ranvir?"

"You look beautiful, Taly, but then you always do."

"You're biased."

"Perhaps, but it's also the truth." Pulling her close, he gently kissed her lips. "I love you, Taly."

"I love you, too. Let's go do this."

∞ ∞ ∞ ∞ ∞

Closing her eyes, Taly took a deep breath and held it for a count of ten before slowly exhaling. It was something she did every time before going on stage. It calmed and centered her, and if there was ever a time she needed it, it was now.

Slowly, she moved across the stage she'd performed on countless times to the nearly invisible spot on the floor that perfectly centered her.

Looking toward the back of the room, her gaze found Vujcec's. "Are you ready?"

"We're ready when you are. Just say when."

"And you've ensured Shui can't shut down the transmission?"

"I've got this thing bouncing off so many relay stations on so many different channels that the only way that would be possible is if he completely shut down the entire Kirs electronic infrastructure, which he'd never do."

"How do you know that?"

"Because if he did, it would shut down *everything*. Communications. Defense. Power. Transit systems. It's all interconnected. Shui demanded it, so he had control. It would take days, maybe weeks, to get everything back up and running. Not even Shui is crazy enough to do that. It would leave him completely vulnerable to attack."

Taly hoped he was right. She took a deep breath and said the word that would forever change her life.

"When."

She looked straight into the red light on the tiny drone hovering several feet in front of her and waited precious seconds. She'd learned the art of a dramatic pause at a young age.

"Hello. In case you don't recognize me, I am Talyani Zulfiqar. A short while ago, many of you saw a recording of me and aren't sure if it was real. I'm here to clear that up along with many other things. Starting with Emperor Shui's claim that I had been abducted.

"I. Was. Not.

"I willingly left Kirs when I learned of the emperor's plot to arrest and imprison innocent citizens because of who their family members and friends were. Those family and friends are cyborgs. The very Kirs citizens who have sacrificed their lives and bodies to protect the rest of us.

"They swore an oath to protect our people from any force that would try and destroy us. They discovered Emperor Shui was doing this by silencing all who disagreed with him."

Taly looked away from the drone for a moment, seemingly to gather her thoughts. When she looked directly into it again, her gaze was hard.

"I was one of those people Shui wanted to silence. Not because I spoke out against him, but because he wanted to use me the way he uses all our people for his own gain. He believed that if I were killed while on Bionus, you, my fans, would rise up and demand retribution. That you would fully support his invasion of a planet that has never been anything but peaceful with Kirs.

"But I didn't go to Bionus as scheduled. I began to hear rumors of the arrests Shui was making. The arrests of innocents. The arrests of cyborgs. The killings of anyone who tried to interfere. All because a cyborg pod refused to carry out the orders they'd been given, to kill innocent citizens.

"Now, you might find this story unbelievable. I know I did when I first heard it. After all, I'm just an entertainer—no one of any real importance. I was then told of a second assassination attempt to occur while visiting the Interplanetary Children's Hospital three weeks ago.

"Do you remember it? A great deal was made about it on the news feeds and social media platforms because General Qubad's grandson was a patient there."

She paused, giving everyone the time to remember. "The hospital was supposed to be leveled, and the attack blamed on the rebels."

Even this deep in space, Taly swore she could hear millions gasp in disbelief.

"I know this because the cyborg ordered to carry out both these attempts told me. How is that possible, you ask? It's possible because, during Shui's trial, I snuck onto one of the prison transport ships." Taly paused, knowing her next words could very well cause her parents' deaths. Still, it needed to be said. "I did this because I have a half-brother, unbeknownst to the rest of Kirs.

"A half-brother that I love very much.

"A half-brother who is a cyborg.

"I wasn't going to let him rot in prison for doing the right thing, for protecting not only me but all of you, from a tyrant. So, I snuck onto the ship I believed he'd be on and waited until the time was right to free him and his pod, but something happened. And not what the emperor told you.

"I was hiding in a maintenance closet when I overheard two guards talking about getting to the escape pods because the ship was set to self-destruct in fifteen minutes, and there was no way to change it. You can imagine my shock. Our emperor, the one so many of you support, or support because you're too afraid not to, planned on murdering thousands upon thousands of citizens right before your eyes.

"Discovering this, I did the only thing I could, the thing I believe every one of you would do in the same situation. I opened the cells and freed the prisoners, giving everyone at least the chance of survival on that transport ship.

"That's how I found myself in an escape pod with five strangers the emperor had branded as rebels, four cyborgs and one civilian. We didn't know one another and had never met before, but we worked together and made our way to my private transport docked on the dark side of Tyurma. We were able to make our escape, but not before helplessly watching as the Kirs military systematically fired on the remaining escape pods."

Taly didn't try to stem the tears streaming down her cheeks. "I have never witnessed such carnage in my life. How evil must a man be to order such a thing? How soulless the ones that carried out such a heinous act.

"As for the cyborg ordered to assassinate me? I now consider him a trusted friend. He was one of the cyborgs seen in the recording on Yelmurn preventing me from leaving the Troubadour. It wasn't because he was kidnapping me. It was because he was protecting me from the bounty hunters chasing me. Bounty hunters the emperor is paying to conceal his murderous crimes.

"So there can be no doubt. No question. I'm stating that I, Talyani Zulfiqar, completely stand with those who stand against Emperor Shui's reign of tyranny. I'm asking you, the citizens of Kirs, Bionus, and every other planet in the universe, to stand with us. To fight with us. To assist those Shui has condemned any way you can.

"One day, I will sing for you again in a free and peaceful world, but until that day, I must do what I can to end this evil. I hope you will join me in making that happen."

∞ ∞ ∞ ∞ ∞

Ranvir stood, utterly stunned by what he had just seen and heard. His Taly had been amazing. She'd just called out Shui in the most public of ways. In a way, Shui couldn't manipulate or change, not the way Vujcec had broadcast it. Kirs was now aware of what Shui had done and was planning on doing.

Would it help the rebellion?

Or had the emperor already crushed it?

Only time would tell.

Touching his earbud, he ordered, "Ganesha, get us out of here."

"With pleasure, Major. Destination?"

"Tuater. Maximum speed."

"You still want to go to Tuater?" Taly asked, walking up to wrap her arms around his waist.

"Yes." Leaning down, he captured her lips for a quick kiss. "It's a good place to hide and rest while we plan our next move. You were amazing up there."

"Was I? There was so much I wanted to say. I'm not sure I got it all in."

"You did," he reassured, leading her out of the concert hall and toward the lower level.

"Where are you taking me?" she asked.

"To the dining room. After all we've been through, we deserve a decent meal."

"I can agree with that. I'll even..." she trailed off as the most fantastic aroma hit her nose. "What's that?"

Entering the dining room, they found Sato just setting down a steaming bowl on a table that already held several platters of food.

"I was just about to comm you," Sato told them.

"You were?" Taly asked.

"Yes," she rubbed her hands on the apron she wore. "I can't do any of the amazing things the rest of you can. I'm just a wife and mother, but I can ensure you're all properly fed."

Walking over to give her a reassuring hug, Taly told her, "You're more than that, Sato. If it wasn't for you, Ranvir and I might never have made it back to the Troubadour. We owe you more than we can ever repay." Sato blushed at the compliment. "And if this food tastes half as good as it smells, then you're the amazing one."

The dining room doors opened and the room filled with the rest of their pod.

"Something smells amazing!" Vujcec announced and headed directly to the table. "I don't know about the rest of you, but after escaping from bounty hunters and calling out an evil emperor, I'm starving."

His antics had everyone laughing. Even Ganesha cracked a smile, and they all moved to the table and sat down, including Ree, holding Uki. Taly looked around.

"Where's Oved?"

"Right here," he said, coming out of the galley carrying a pitcher of drinks.

"Great, now we can eat." Taly looked to Sato. "Sit down, Sato. You're not our servant."

"I..." Oved put a gentle hand on his wife's arm and guided her to the seat next to Ree.

As the pod ate, back in Taly's quarters the comm station signaled an incoming transmission.

About the Author

Michelle has always loved to read, and writing is just a natural extension of this for her. Growing up, she loved to extend the stories of books she'd read to see where the characters went. Happily married for over thirty years, she is the proud mother of two grown children and a grandmother of three beautiful grandchildren. You can reach her at m.k.eidem@live.com or visit her website at http://www.mkeidem.com for upcoming books.

Additional Books

Cassandra's Challenge: The Challenge Series, Book 1

Victoria's Challenge: The Challenge Series, Book 2

Jacinda's Challenge: The Challenge Series, Book 3

Stephanie's Challenge: The Challenge Series, Book 4

Grim: Tornians Book 1

A Grim Holiday: Tornians Book 2

Wray: Tornians Book 3

Ynyr: Tornians Book 4

Oryon: Tornians Book 5

A Grim Pet: Tornians Book 6

Ull: Tornians Book 7

A Grim Baby: Book 8

Nikhil: Kaliszians Book 1

Treyvon: Kaliszians Book 2

Kirall's Kiss: Kiss Series Book 1

Autumn's Kiss: Kiss Series Book 2

Supreme's Kiss: Kiss Series Book 3

Her Commanders (Stand Alone)

Foreign Language (Italiano)

Grim: Tornians Italiano Vol. 1

Una Grim Vacanza: Tornians Italiano Vol. 2

Wray: Tornians Italiano Vol. 3

Foreign Language (Français)

Le Baiser de Kirall (La série des Baisers T.1)

Le Baiser d'Autumn (La série des Baisers T.2)

Le Baiser Suprême (La série des Baisers T.3)

Grim: Tornians Livre 1

Des Fêtes Grim: Tornians Livre 2

Wray: Tornians Livre 3

CPSIA information can be obtained
at www.ICGtesting.com
Printed in the USA
LVHW041639060722
722768LV00003B/61